D0952694

EITHER THE BEGINNING OR THE END OF THE WORLD

It is either the beginning or the end
of the world, and the choice is ourselves
or nothing.

—Carolyn Forché,
"Ourselves or Nothing"

EITHER THE BEGINNING OR THE END OF THE WORLD

TERRY FARISH

Carolrhoda Lab™
An imprint of Carolrhoda Books
A division of Lerner Publishing Group, Inc.
241 First Avenue North
Minneapolis, MN 55401 USA

For reading levels and more information,
look up this title at www.lernerbooks.com.

The images in this book are used with the permission of: © Jonas Elmqvist/Nordic Photos/Getty Images (window frame); © Diana Berlizeva/EyeEm/Getty Images (frosted glass).

Main body text set in Janson Text LT Std 10/14.
Typeface provided by Linotype AG.

Library of Congress Cataloging-in-Publication Data

Farish, Terry.
Either the beginning or the end of the world / by Terry Farish.
pages cm
Summary: Sofie, sixteen, lives alone with her father, a Scottish fisherman, on New Hampshire's coast and is not prepared for the return of her pregnant mother, a Cambodian immigrant, or for the forbidden relationship she has begun with a young Army medic back from Afghanistan.
ISBN 978-1-4677-7483-3 (lb : alk. paper) — ISBN 978-1-4677-8813-7 (EB pdf)
[1. Single-parent families—Fiction. 2. Fishing—Fiction. 3. Cambodian Americans—Fiction. 4. Racially mixed people—Fiction. 5. Veterans—Fiction. 6. Secrets—Fiction. 7. New Hampshire—Fiction.] I. Title.
PZ7.F22713Eit 2015
[Fic]—dc23 2015001606

Manufactured in the United States of America
2—BP—2/1/16

For Ty

Lullaby

Ma sings to me, her long hair flowing.
I love her more than the dark loves dawn.
She was sixteen. She sang to me.
We climb above the water while she sings her baby song.
When the moon draws the water, Ma draws me too.
And she draws her small brother.
My family rides in the curve of the moon.

—Sofie Grear

FEBRUARY 28

Luke and I have plans like deer in winter have plans. The trees are bare. The moon is full. We could shelter in place. We could run.

The cabin looks out to the rocky Atlantic coast, and tonight you'd think the wind and the waves could wash the very boulders back into the sea.

I know Luke has barely seen his family since he came back from Afghanistan, where he served with the New Hampshire Army National Guard. I have seen his mother's texts. I saw a photo she sent of Luke's little sister in a white angel gown in front of a Christmas tree. The child has a gleeful gap-toothed grin, her little white-sleeved arms crossed over the gown's pink inlay, and curls spiraling from beneath her tiara. She holds a sign in crayon letters. I made you pancakes do you remember me? mandy *Sometimes I can hear his mother crying out from her texts*—lucas, call us day or night—*and I feel sad for her.*

"What if we go away from here?" I say. "From the ocean." It's nearly midnight, but the wind gusting makes us vigilant. I look up from the edge of the bed, where I sit. Luke paces as if to ensure that he doesn't close his eyes.

He says, "That's most of the country." I grin, but I begin to shake in the night chill of this bare winter rental. He stops. Kicks up the fire in the woodstove. Comes to me. Buttons my sweater against the cold. To take in each other's eyes would break us down. His hand pauses at my hip. I touch his dark hair. We are framed by the window covered in crystals of ice.

If I go, I would leave my father. I see him outlined as simply as a boat on the horizon beside a red ball of sun. My father always says he loves to go fishing to see the red ball of sun rise out of the water.

I get out my phone, and Luke and I check Google Maps for some of the places we've pretended we'd go. We sit cross-legged on his squealing bed. Our foreheads touch. We make up stories about us living here, together. We have a cupboard with cereal bowls and a drawer with spoons tucked in each other.

Wherever we are, I know he'll have the gun.

My shaking is so bad, my teeth tap against each other. I wrap the thin bedspread around us. My dog, Pilot, sleeps by the stove in a knot she's made of my coat, which she dragged there.

"What do you have against the ocean?" Luke says. His voice is tight but unrushed. I think we are both acutely aware of everything. A flicker of light from a buoy in the distance, when Pilot circles, drops down again. Is it like the talk before soldiers go on patrol? This is a part of him I try to imagine. "You're a fishing family," he says. "I don't understand."

We're just telling stories. Now I look at him.

I can't see the green of his eyes. His face is an outline. I need his voice to hold on to who he really is. But I feel his calm. He always says he's most steady in chaos. "My mother says I came out stillborn because of a curse from the Pol Pot time. But I took this big gasping breath, and all the Cambodian side of my family was there and they all breathed with me."

My breath is shallow as I tell this. It aches to breathe.

"I don't trust the ocean," I say. "It knows. It's beautiful and it calls me. It suspects I'm really a stillborn."

Luke nods. I can make him out now. I cock my head to study his unflinching eyes. I thought this would make sense to him, since he talks to dead people he knew from the army. I touch his ribs beneath the thick yarn of his sweater. "Superstitious fisherman's kid." I shrug, pushing my hair off my face. Then I sit still except for my tapping teeth and let the sound of the waves fill my body. He's lean like a wild dog. We should eat.

If I go, I'll leave my mother. Since I met Luke, I've remembered a song she sang to me when I was little. She sang about a rabbit in the moon, and I became the rabbit in my child imagination, and she became the moon. Later, when I didn't see her, I remembered her long hair, how I used to twist it in my hands as I made little words and pretended I could sing them in Khmer.

I love you more than the dark loves dawn.
You were sixteen. You sang to me.
We climb above the water while you sing your baby song.

"Couple a loonies," Luke says over the banging in the wind of the loose cabin window.

"But you're used to me," I say.

"Christ help me," he says.

I say, "Me too."

We are dangerous. We have warned each other about this. Part of him is stillborn too. "Some things you shouldn't know." He often wishes this for me about what happened in his war. We've tried to protect each other since we met. But here we are together by the open sea.

PIRATES

When the January catch is slim in the Gulf of Maine and my father can't pay for even the fuel for the *Karma*, rumble begins about taking the boat down to Chincoteague. *Maybe in the spring,* he and some other fishermen begin to say. *When shrimping's done, maybe it's time to go to Chincoteague.* Virginia's a distance from New Hampshire, but there he can fish—groundfishing, for monkfish that have teeth like a shark.

It's just my father and me in our family. My mother has never lived with us, though I have a memory of living with her and my grandmother in a room with long windows in Lowell, Massachusetts.

This spring, if my father goes to Chincoteague, I know he will not take a sixteen-year-old, me, his only daughter. But we're a team. I hold bear-tight to winter.

As the cold encases our small house, among all the row houses by the river, I'm aware of the glitter on snow lit by the moon. I let my eyes follow up and search for the rabbit in the moon's lines and bumps. My father says no other fishermen do this, just us. Rabbit running. Rabbit stirring a pot with a long spoon. Rabbit with one ear up, one ear down. I'm usually aware of the moon like I'm usually aware of how much the birch trees bend, a way that I can judge the velocity of the wind. That's how I know if my father will go fishing, if the boat can handle in the sea. That's how I can predict his return.

No moon shines this January night. It starts to snow at dinnertime.

My father is on the phone while I chop a white onion and drop the bits to spit in hot oil.

Pilot thumps her tail on the wood floor like a drum, ever hopeful for scraps when I cook. My father holds the phone to his ear over the bandana he ties around his forehead and his shaggy hair. Whoever he called must not have answered.

"Sleep in," he says into the phone. "We'll wait out the storm."

I stir milk into the sizzling onion and chunks of fish and simmer our chowder. I'm suddenly aware that my finger is bare, no ring spins around. My tiger's eye. Somewhere, it slipped off. *Your only good taste in fashion*, my friend Rosa teases me about my ring, and it's from my dad.

We're not too big on fashion here. Dad says if I come at him sideways he'd miss me anyway. Boots, jeans tucked in. Year round. Keeps you ready. The ones at the Goodwill have creases and life. The rest of me is still unplanned. Rosa says I'm trending, though, a kind of fisherman–co-op–rat look. Snarled sweaters. Stocking caps over thick, wound-around hair.

Noticing my hand, though, I miss my ring something awful. I don't like me bare.

Snow falls faster. Hard snow. The outdoor spotlight shines on my father's tower of lobster traps. In twenty minutes the traps disappear under snow. Snow flies into the window glass, fast, heavy, and silent.

My father still wears his rubber knee-high boots, his plaid shirt—the cuffs rolled, showing the veins and muscles in his arms. I pull two bowls off the shelf and dig the ladle from among the spoons, beaters, scrapers in the drawer.

"Was that the new deckhand?"

My father had mentioned somebody who'd been crewing with him.

"Yeah," he says. "Good crew."

I scoop steaming chowder into our bowls. My father lowers his body into the chair. Curls of pale hair hang down from beneath his bandana and graze his long neck. I adore his face, pocked with scars from snapped lines and hard work on the sea.

My mother has black hair that her mother tied in a scarf when they lived in Cambodia. My eyes are my mother's. We have identical dark eyes, almost black. If people should see us, no one would miss that we're mother and child.

My father and I settle into the chowder. We eat with big spoons and break off hunks of biscuit to dunk in. He says, "I leave you on your own too much, Sofie."

I scowl. "'Cause of the gin! Dad, I should have made you ground me, right then."

Rosa and I got into his gin. She's into classic country, and she was playing a song Emmylou Harris sings, and I twirled while she played. Rosa said we looked so silly-drunk, no story would save us. But when my father walked in the door, he said, "Where's the supper?" That's all he said.

"What about the gin?" he asks while we're trying to eat chowder. "Jesus." He does not want to think about gin or teenaged girls. He is in over his head with fatherhood. Forgetting to set curfews. Not a clue. I should have said, *Dad, I'm grounded until I tell you when.*

My father turns the problem of boys into our standing joke. He often tells me, "You can always come home. No matter what." This is delivered in the open doorway, his long arms stretched wide, hands above the doorframe, to me as I head out the door to the grocery store, to school, to Rosa's. I glance back, deadpan, at his laughing eyes. Shake my head. He is my world. We know. We don't talk about these things. Boys. Girls with boys.

But usually we're golden. We deal with school—the rolling routines, deadlines we can predict. My teachers ask about him. The last of the fishermen, my teacher Mr. Murray calls him. I wonder what they see when they see a slow-talking, slow-walking man with the sureness of the sea who is raising a daughter alone.

Again, I imagine my mother. Her black hair is knotted together like my grandmother's as they lean in to eat their supper, which includes basmati rice and some kind of fish sauce. I remember the sweet rice and sharp smells of coriander, garlic, and lime. My mother is gauzy to me. She floats like a ghost. My father tells stories in which she's the heartbreak, dark-haired and lovely. To me she is as unreliable as the wind. I grew up and became a tall Scottish girl—my father's side—who chanced to have Cambodian eyes. Does my father see my mother when he looks at me?

I cock my head at my father and tie a kitchen towel around my forehead like his bandana. Two pirates. I tease and smirk and let my long hair sway. I go back to the language my father and I talk.

"I'm not alone," I say. "Pilot and I have our own beach. I know the river as well as the seals, where the good sunning rocks are at low tide." I start off trying to tease about the river, his and mine. We love it the same. "How the river narrows—how it gets a funnel like a snake in the middle—and rips back out to the ocean." But his lips are taut. His face won't soften. I end, unsure, "Who's alone?"

My father works his forehead with his wide, calloused hand. "I want to do right by you, Sofie." He turns his blue eyes on me.

"You *always* do right." I hear my own voice, too urgent.

"I try to act on my instincts, not knowing how things are going to come out. Sometimes it's against any common sense. Sometimes it doesn't seem right."

I can see it in the curve of his lips when the wolf comes knocking. Sometimes he sings me lines from his favorite Springsteen songs for the worry. But now he's not singing, and the worry's too heavy to fix. I gather the spoons and bowls.

"Got homework," I sing.

"Sit down," my father says.

"What?" I say.

"After shrimping, I'm going down to Chincoteague . . ."

Not maybe.

"When I go," he finishes, "your mother's going to stay here a while."

My head whips around toward him as if something had slammed against my cheekbone, and my father gets his look of tragic amusement. This look, like a shield, always comes when he mentions my mother and me. He takes the bowls to the sink. Then he fishes his glasses from his shirt pocket and sits on the couch with the newspaper. But he keeps saying words.

"I can't leave you alone here."

"Coming *here*! My mother?"

"You might see something of your grandmother, too."

A flash of my grandmother's angry bird eyes and bent, yellow fingers that scared me. The smell of turmeric. My father folds the newspaper back against itself. Pilot sits on her haunches, tense with the drama.

I am frozen.

I pull off the pirate towel.

"Sofie . . ." he begins. "What I'm saying is, she could use a place, and I have to go south where I can catch some fish. Fishermen got the wolf at the door."

I knew it was about the wolf.

I swing open the back door. I stand by my father's orange oils that hang on the doorframe. The pants drip and make a puddle on the linoleum. I step through the piles of yellow traps, the rusted iron pots on the back steps, the transmission parts, past the blue skiff propped against the brick chimney.

Tears stream down my face, and I taste salt and onion. Pilot licks my salted fingers. When the ache from the cold is too much I come back inside to the woodstove. My father glances over his tan-framed Walmart glasses. "It's something we got to think about. A girl needs to know her mother."

I shout, "Stop!" I just need him to stop talking. It is completely offensive, my shouting, since my father is steady like a boat in calm waters. And he loves me. My mother gave me away. I am accustomed to aching for her and hating her. I never ever want to see her again after what she did to my father and me.

WHILE WE MEND NETS

Later that night, when I can't stop my mind from spinning, I come down the dark stairs with Pilot so close behind I can feel her head against my thighs. I want my father to say, *Got it covered. All's well.* But when I get to the living room, he's standing at the window in the dark, talking to someone on his cell. He is silent. The occasional low *yup, all right.* Someone else is talking. He never talks on the phone, except to check in with crew. He never listens in the dark.

I stay in the shadows on the stairs. I feel Pilot's heartbeat as she leans into me.

The beating wind fades, then comes around. It has a steady rhythm, like my father and me when we work on the nets. We weave twine through the shrimp nets, pulling the shuttles through as we weave the torn parts tight. Row after row after row. Sometimes nets cover our living room, drape over furniture, as we work and wait for shrimp season to open.

Fishing is a family business. When he's groundfishing, my father steams five, six hours off shore to Platts Bank, Jeffrey's Ledge, Fippennies. I enter tiny numbers in our log to keep track of what he puts into the *Karma* and what she brings back from the sea. I'm also in charge of grocery coupons. This morning I'd found a soap coupon, *Buy one, get one free.* That's why at this moment in the dark we both smell like the same floral soap I found on sale.

Months ago, at Thanksgiving time, while we worked on the nets, the wolf came up, like it does. I'd said, "I'm old enough for the business." He'd said, "Somebody around here got to have a head for it. You're the boss."

Then we heard the sound of helicopter rotors. The sound continued for hours as a helicopter hovered over the river, searching the water on either side of the Piscataqua River Bridge. This has happened more than one time since my father and I moved to the Heights. Our house is a row house, one of the small brick houses built before the first World War for shipbuilders and their families on the river. The sound of the rotors plying the river slowed our hands as we worked.

Eventually my father had left the nets and the twine and sat in the growing dark beside the woodstove. I wished the helicopter would pull away and hush. They would stop if the search crew found what had fallen into the river. Or jumped into the river. *Poor bastard*, was all my father said. But he couldn't work, and I knew he was shaken by whoever it was whose life hurt him so badly that he had come to a bridge with a 135-foot clearance below at high tide. Add another 9 feet at low tide. My father had laid his hand on my head.

But now no reassurance comes. No hand on my head. No hug to his shaggy hair. I stay in the shadows at the bottom of the stairs, already knowing, not taking the chance.

But if he'd just turn. Give me a look of shared confidence—my father in his bandana and me, the girl he swore he'd die for—the exotic-looking one, strangers probably say when they meet us. His daughter's got those dark, swimming eyes.

Like I'm from some Asian war nobody clearly remembers.

BRIDGE

The Piscataqua River Bridge rises and arches like an enormous heron, its wings wide in flight.

In the morning Pilot and I follow our unplowed street to the river path, then slog through the snow to our stretch of beach beneath the bridge. I barely see its shape in the morning dark, even now that I'm standing beside it. But I know the wings of the bridge curve out to the sky. Suddenly Pilot bays a high, chilling animal alarm. Nobody hangs out here. Especially in cold so fierce a body could crack. But I see a person in the snowy dawn, balanced on one of the rusted I-beams of a pier that was once here, maybe destroyed by the fast-running river. At low water the narrow beams reach long, first over rocks and then the river. Who'd want to be so near thirty-five-degree water screaming by?

His feet are wide. A him?

Pilot races in a wide arc around him. "Pilot," I call softly. She is black and invisible in this light, except for her feet, which are white. I can't find her feet running. Then a strip of pink light shows between the river and the sky. She's there. A black cartoon nearly grown puppy with a licorice tail. The person turns, a figure etched in the new light, unaware of me.

I make out camouflage baggy pants. Boots. A muddy-colored cap pulled low.

Soldier things. The soldier shifts his feet on the beam like it's a tightrope. I drop to the sand and hold out my arms. Pilot's bony frame slams in. I fix on the marks on the soldier's clothes and the cap that covers his eyes. His shoulders sag. He holds something in his right hand, his far hand from me. The sun's pink tinge creeps through the mist and out of the water. The sun!

My beach is not long, just the rocky shore you can walk at low tide between the bridge to the east and woods of white birch and oaks to the west. I'm not twenty feet from him. I call "Hey" toward the pier. He doesn't say "Hey" back.

Everything's different this morning. It's a school day. And I'm here, and there's a soldier in the silver light. After what my father said last night.

Pilot escapes my reach again. She gives out a ridiculously deep bark for the baby she is, all eleven months of her, a gangly puppy with pancake-sized feet.

The soldier moves.

"She's friendly," I say.

Pilot calls up a gravelly howl from deep inside her. The soldier finally turns his head toward us. The soldier's right hand seems to tremble and drum against his leg. Pilot's body shakes with concentration on his every move. The pink light streaks over the sky. The soldier's head bends at a funny angle, and for some reason I think of the Tin Man.

"I'm not going to hurt her," the soldier says. "The dog." He scatters his words into the cold air. I glance at him directly. I see more of his face in the new light.

Pilot sprawls flat, from muzzle to tail, watching him. "You're on her beach," I say.

A low sound comes out of the soldier. It isn't worried like Pilot's. It's flat.

Pilot lets out a yip that cuts through the cold. "Excuse me," I say, "do you have any treats? She's food motivated. That's what they said at the shelter. If you had a treat, she might stop howling."

Looking at the soldier, I don't think he's much older than Jamie, next door, who turned nineteen in December. He wears a thick watchband with a face as wide as his wrist. An American flag is stitched on his shoulder, only it's in black and white. His lips are small, straight lines, except for a part that's bloody and swollen. I want to tell him, *Stay away from the Page. People get shot in that bar.*

Was he a soldier in Afghanistan? With Mr. Murray we are studying the country the way it was before we were at war.

The soldier gets the word *treat*. Finally he pats his chest pockets. His hip pockets. He even has pockets on his sleeves. Above the flag are stripes like arrows.

If he answers I don't know. The roar of traffic from the bridge sucks up any words.

Finally the soldier comes up with a packet of airline peanuts from one of his millions of pockets. "She like peanuts?" I think he says. He doesn't focus on either of us.

"Her name's Pilot," I say. "Call her."

The birches moan when the trees lean into each other, and then the wind suddenly stops. The soldier lets out a long, quivery whistle. It's as if he heard a command—call her—and obeys.

Pilot lifts her sleek self, walks straight to him. She scarfs up every peanut he holds out in his hand, then licks the scent from his open palm.

My eyes are drawn to a glint of light, something in his other hand. I take a step nearer. But the soldier does some kind of trick, pulling something from another pocket. I freeze. I see what he drops into a place beneath his coat. What had glinted in the sunlight shining through falling snow was a gun.

The warnings my mother would try to scare me with flash in my mind. Danger is everywhere. Trust no one. The spirits will get you. They want to take you to live with them. Watch out for spirits on your path. They lie in wait. For you, Sophea.

I am not afraid. I don't know any Khmer Rouge or the Pol Pot time my grandmother talked about. I am not Cambodian. I am

American. *I am not afraid.* I have no past. I have no ancestors. I have no mother. I make myself from scratch every day.

"Found this hanging from the fence." The soldier gestures to the cyclone fence that divides the woods from the riverbank. My eyes leave his face and glance at what he holds. My ring. The black slit in the tiger's eye stone gleams. He holds it out to me. I am aware of the ring, the rock, the soldier, the sun, the moon sucking the river back into the sea.

"That's mine." I find myself shouting at him, as if he'll pull the ring back and pocket it, too.

He tosses it, and it lands in the crevice of the rock at my feet. On my knees, I scoop it into my hands clumsy with thick mittens.

He's watching me. "Are you real?" he asks.

Somehow, this is confusing. I wrap my arms around myself. "I don't know."

But all of a sudden, I'm aware of being a physical person. I'm aware of the ribbing of my undershirt hugging my wrists. I'm aware of my hair I wound in my fist that falls to the nape of my neck under my stocking cap. I feel the cold air as I breathe into my chest. We squint our eyes in the shard of sunlight and take each other in.

"What's your name?" I say. Did he forget the gun inside his coat?

"Luke. Lucas."

I see the shadow of his beard. I step back.

"I'm Sofie." I jerk Pilot, who wants to run. Then I let her go and she flies, her floppy ears thrown back like Superman capes. I wonder what color his eyes are. Maybe, like the river, they change with the angle of light. I love the feel of my ring back with me in my fist. It feels solid. I feel solid. But I can't keep it.

I open my mitten with my ring. "My father gave me this," I say. "I'm giving it back to you. It's for good luck, wherever you're going. It's a tiger's eye."

I come closer, balance the ring on the steel bar. But this time I stay and study the American flag high up on his sleeve and try to make out the patch beneath it. Something *Army National Guard. New Hampshire.* I see a patch shaped like a shield, with many stars. Nine. Beneath that, bright colored bars. Striped and starred. Why did he pin on all these badges to stand under a roaring bridge?

"How old are you?" he asks.

"Sixteen," I say, not thinking, since I'm almost seventeen. "Seventeen," I say, but the roar of six lanes of cars overhead flattens it.

The soldier lifts his glasses and turns his eyes on me. They are yellow-green exhausted eyes that are both terrifying and beckoning. I feel like I'm wearing nothing but the cotton undershirt and he can see every bone up my rib cage. "You need a night's sleep," I say, and again I feel the fear in my legs and also fascination with his eyes. He looks at me with eyes that make me remember lines my father used to tell me from a Scottish nursery rhyme. It begins, *One for sorrow.* I'm stalled on the first line.

I say, "I have to go."

He pulls back toward the river.

But he tosses something quite light toward me, and I catch it. It jangles on a silver chain that slides between my mittens. What is this? In exchange for the ring? I wrap it in my hand.

"Sofie Grear!" I hear from the trees. My dog stops tearing across the strip of beach where, at the horizon, the splotch of pink shows through the snow clouds. She listens, too. "Sofie." Short. Abrupt. It's my father. He sees the soldier on the steel beam. I hold what the soldier tossed out of sight. Overhead, the sky has become smoke.

"Sofie, come away from there." I hear tension in my father's voice. My father with the calmness of the sea.

"I'm not a lost dog," I call.

Without looking, I feel the soldier—Luke—straighten.

My father drops down through the scrub brush to the rocky

beach so quickly, it's as if he thought the current of the river had sucked me into her snake body. High above, angles and lines of the bridge disappear in the fog and the snow.

"Sofie," he calls again.

"I'm here."

"What are you, crazy?" I am still near the beam. For one second my father looks like he is going to come hard on the soldier, and I think of the silly joke we have, "You can always come home. No matter what." *I could always come home.* What is there in the world to keep me from my father?

But the soldier and I are here in the snow. It's hard to place my father here.

It's Luke who jumps from the pier to the rocky beach. He speaks softly, and my father answers in such a way that I realize they know each other. Luke looks at my father, his face at an angle. He is deferential. He holds out his hand. He wants to shake my father's hand. My father extends his hand a short way to be done with the business of greeting, but Luke takes his hand in both of his. Then he leaps across the rocks and disappears into the snow.

I slide the silver chain into my pocket.

A MILLION SUNS

The sun had risen and bloomed for only a second in the sky. Pilot and I climb the steep path slippery with snow back up into the evergreen woods, up to the trail that follows the cyclone fence for a few yards where Luke found my ring. I try to run through the deep snow. I'm not ready to talk to my father. I imagine the school bus horn honking, a world away. Everything feels mysterious and foreign. The snow has become glitter. Glitter falls on Pilot's ears as I pound through the snow off the trail.

"What were you doing?" My father is beside me.

"You know him." It sounds like an accusation. Why am I so angry?

"What did you think you were doing!"

"What do you mean? I wasn't doing anything." We trudge in silence through the thorny branches, curved low under the weight of snow. Snow sticks to my clothes. Pine boughs make the woods smell like Christmas. The air is so cold, clouds of our breath rise. We can see each other's streams of smoke.

"You're stepping where you don't belong." His face is tight with cold and something like fear. "You have your whole life ahead of you."

"What did I do? I was talking to him."

"Sofie, you're too young."

"I'm sixteen. Wasn't my mother sixteen?"

"Your mother was . . ." He doesn't have the words.

"I have to go to school."

"There is no school. This is a storm."

This stops me and brings me back to my father. I almost drop down and hug his knees like a child. What if he'd gone out, and instead of us yelling at each other in the woods like we're doing, he'd be trying to fix the transmission or whatever broke on a boat taking on water in fifty-knot winds. I have nightmares about this. Storms are my nightmares. Fisherman's daughter dreams.

But he's here. I slow down. I stop trying to escape him.

A million tiny suns repeat on a boulder ahead from the glare of the shard of sun.

Where's the soldier? Luke. Thinking of him is like startling awake. He ran from the beach and into the snow. Someone needs to take the gun away. Maybe he has gone somewhere to sleep—his eyes were exhausted—and I will approach, careful not to crunch on the snow or scatter the beach stones underfoot. And I'll steal the gun away. I will carry it in two hands, pointing down.

All this is in my imagination while my father and I trudge through the snow, together, bits of fire coming from our breath.

"Sofie, keep away from that kid." My father's voice is too loud.

I ask, "How do you know him?"

"He crewed for me. I know him. Just out of the service. You stay away from him."

"You're going to Chincoteague. You're leaving me with my mother."

"If I don't land the fish, what kind of business are you going to run?"

Important things are not said, like the secret I know about the soldier. The gun he slid maybe into a holster inside his coat.

The *you're too young*. Like my mother? Why's my mother different? Tell me what you know.

The *are you real?* The question the soldier asked me. I still feel it in my body.

Pilot and I walk ahead. I am imagining the blast of the gun.

My father has a gun. A lot of fishermen do. He taught me how to fire it. He taught me how to steady a gun. He taught me how to clasp my left hand around my firing hand holding the gun, stop breathing, and fire.

But in my mind I see this gun and the hands of the soldier in a January dawn . . . alone. The gun in his own hand. *Click click click baam.* A horrible flash—a boy's, a young man's body—his blood washing into the river. A boy who searched his pockets for peanuts for my dog.

I need to see you, I think, *so I can take this image away.*

KILIM

I tell Rosa that my father is going to Chincoteague. I don't tell her that he says my mother is coming to my house. I don't want this to happen. I have no place in my head to even talk about it. I want to talk about the boy who crews for my father, Luke, who I met by chance on my beach.

"I shouldn't see him," I tell Rosa.

She watches me, excited, since I've never been interested in anybody. I like running cross-country with boys. I like laughing and racing through the woods and dancing rock to rock, forging streams and collapsing under trees with them. They're my friends. Sometimes Rosa tries to match me up, but I never would.

She's the party girl. She calls me driven.

"I have to see him," I say.

"Are you looking for advice?" she asks.

"No."

She shrugs, and the tassels on the white hat she wears swirl playfully like a child's hat. We're red-cheeked with cold, even inside our meeting place, Caffe Kilim. Each time the door opens, we shiver. *Before* the door opens, we shiver and brace ourselves.

I glance around the coffee shop. "Don't lecture," I say, "about how I always said no boys."

"As long as you don't lecture me."

"You broke up? Again?"

"He didn't *get* me. I always had to finish my sentences."

We laugh. This makes perfect sense to us.

"You want a person to *get* you," she elaborates. "I'd never say to you, come on, Sofie, let's spend the day at Wallis Sands in the waves. You don't go in the ocean. Like I can't look down from the bridge. How could anybody jump? They'd have to get up there."

So we agree. We're perfect. To each other.

Kilim smells like coffee beans, like our whole tourist town. Brianna behind the counter lifts the lid of the milk steamer. She pours foam over the bitter coffee in an orange and black Kilim cardboard cup. Boats at the Fisherman's Co-op are littered with orange and black cups. Brianna, silver bangles on her tattooed arms, cuts the foam in midstream. They don't make nonpaying customers leave.

"How are you going to find him?" she asks.

"I don't think I'll have to. It'll happen." I say this without thinking.

My mind goes back to the co-op, where I had waited for Rosa. Ducks with emerald heads swarmed the pier. A new boat was berthed there, *Storm Rider*. My father wasn't there. The harbor was quiet. Not a single fisherman was out there working on his boat in the punishing, aching cold. The boats hugged the pier even while waves rolled and tossed them.

"Before you came, my eyes did funny things," I tell Rosa. "I imagined the soldier was on *Storm Rider*, and he was thrown flat on the deck. And I got scared and didn't know if I could . . ." Rosa can't finish this one. She watches me. "If I could . . . leave. I'd want to stay."

"I can't believe this is you talking," she says.

I rub my arms in the cold and press my lips at the enormous mystery. Being drawn to somebody so much, he is even in the circles my breath makes on the windowpane.

Rosa buttons her coat to the tip of her chin. "Your father will lock you on board the *Karma*, even with your ocean phobia, and you'll spend your youth at sea." A sly smile.

I want to tell her we might need to worry about how much I want to see him.

I still don't mention the gun. I lean into the window seat at Kilim, my knee on a magazine with a Dolce & Gabbana ad. I keep watch for my father approaching the door. My glance roams up the wall of postcards sent to Kilim from customers on their travels and honeymoons. A kid at the next table holds a paperback open in one hand. The name Rumi crosses the spine beside the bend of his finger.

I let myself look at Rosa again. Lipstick shimmers on her lips. I am relieved. She is real. I am real. I tell her about Pilot streaking across the riverbank. I tell about the flag on the soldier's arm. But in my mind I see the flash of glare off the gun and the gun sliding under his coat. I put my hand in my pocket and pull up the silver chain.

"What's that?"

"He gave it to me."

I open my palm. In it are two small metal rectangles imprinted with the name *Sanna, Lucas.* I trace the bumpy letters.

"His dog tags?" she says.

My hand is wet with sweat.

I can't remember not having Rosa for a friend. When Rosa plays her guitar, for those moments, she takes me to a different world where I'm safe. She plays, I sing. Or I play and sing. We dream up fantasies about being a girl band. Since we were Fisherman's Co-op rats together as kids, she's been my friend.

My father says about me, *This one's a shore girl.* Bad luck on a boat, he means, ever since the time I nearly drowned. Rosa and I were swimming on a wave, into my father's arms. But I had stopped breathing. He thought he'd drowned me. He told me I was still as a corpse, my black hair among the tendrils of seaweed and coated in sand. He turned me on my side to expel the sea from my lungs. I gagged, and the sea came up and I started bawling and rolled into his chest. He rocked me on the beach, and it seemed like days I cried, in a ball against him under a glinting sun and Rosa patting my foot. That's how my father tells it.

"I wanted to be a seal," I told them.

He said, "You're no seal. Stay out of the water. Best you stay off the boat. This one can go on the boat." He meant Rosa. And from then on, I lost trust in the water.

But one summer Rosa and I painted *The Sofie & Rosa* on the *Karma*'s hull. Good ring to it, Dad had said, but it's bad luck to change the name of a boat, so we had to change it back. Fishermen are superstitious. But Rosa and I liked how our names looked on the hull, and that's as close as we got so far to being a girl band.

Rosa takes the dog tags. Holds them in her palms. "You know what you're doing," she says. "You always have." She drops the tags back in my hand. She trusts me.

I want to say, *I do not know what I'm doing.* A chill travels through me. She draws her hands back.

I stand. I take in all the usual things at Kilim's. *Unattended children will be given espresso and a free puppy.* The sign's been there since I can remember. The smell of hot chocolate, the notes on the wall. *I'll give: deep muscle massage For your: used fridge. Homemade Pies for Your Party. Deck Hand*, and a number, in jagged black letters, *Atlantic Co., Local broker buying fresh caught landings. Excellent Prices.*

I am sailing away. *Rosa, hold on to me*, I want to say. Rosa wraps herself with scarves. I zip myself in my father's red quilted jacket. I have always worn his jackets. Am I like my dog? Pilot makes a nest of my shirts and boots—my *boots.* I laugh when I try to picture her hauling my boot into a sunspot so she can sleep when I'm gone. She doesn't chew it, just rests her forehead in the curve of the leather.

"Rosa, wouldn't it be fun if we went to Chincoteague with my father? Do you want to come? Dad said they live on BBQ chicken and beer in the Motel 6. Or we can eat popcorn from the 7-Eleven. Sound good?"

"Outstanding," she says. "And Mr. Murray." We like our World Civ teacher. "What if we kidnap Mr. Murray? Do you think he'd mind? He'd be fun to have on a trip."

I'm picturing all of us squeezing in at the Motel 6. "Our problems are solved," I say. "Wait till I tell my father we're all coming."

"I didn't have any problems until your dad had to leave," Rosa says.

"Except how to get hired at the Press Room to play a few songs."

We decide we'll work on that when we get to Chincoteague. How to break into music in Portsmouth, New Hampshire.

We walk out, and our silly fantasy makes me homesick for being on Chincoteague with Rosa and Mr. Murray, where none of us has ever been. Rosa doesn't mention this is the opposite of finding the soldier. If she had, I couldn't explain. We walk along Islington Street through a tunnel of snow, holding tight to each other's arms.

SECRETS

Under streetlights, a snowplow shapes a narrow crescent around the curve of our street in Atlantic Heights. In the woods between our rows of houses and the bridge, pine boughs bend down, laden with snow. I see no path to the river. No trace of anyone ever walking through the deep snow and into the woods. Where would the soldier have gone? I wonder where he sleeps.

I imagine the soldier with his yellow-green eyes weighted down with snow—like the trees—emerging from the woods. I want to keep talking with him, to tell him, *"My mother is coming to live with me, after all my life of forgetting she has me."* I imagine his eyes and straight lips. He's listening to me. I imagine if I touched him. Just my palm. To his arm. *"My father says a girl needs to know her mother,"* I would tell him. *"But what does he know about girls? He just knows about everything else. He knows about fish."*

Just then my father's truck rattles around the curve. I stay busy, shoveling out the front doorway. His door squeals opens. Slams.

"You going to work?" he calls. "You need the truck?"

"Tomorrow and Friday," I say. The reminder of the smell of pumpkin spice lattes at work makes me queasy.

My father begins to shovel the snow that all but buries the towers of traps, the porch steps, and the driveway. Pilot races to the top and bottom of the crescent path. I help dig out the driveway to make room for the truck, then I dig out the path and stone steps to the porch. Layer by layer I take off clothes as I work till I'm down to my sweaty shirt. I heave shovelfull by shovelfull, getting clammy with sweat, my arms gone weak. But this is better than making lattes at Dunkin' Donuts.

I wish I could race into the woods and on to the little beach on the river. But the path is snowed in, and we are snowed in.

My father fries up chicken and mashes potatoes, my favorite meal. While he cooks, I rekindle the fire in the woodstove. We don't talk. His shoulders round over the stove as he turns the chicken in the skillet. They seem to sag like an old man's shoulders. For a second I imagine him old in his plaid work shirt, bent over from the toll fishing takes on a body, like our friend Pete. He's got fingers permanently bent back, a big scar above his eye, knees that don't bend right so he shuffles. The image of my dad that way makes me wince.

My father and I thaw out our achy hands and feet at the woodstove. He serves up the chicken and substantial gravy over our potatoes with the skin. I save most of mine for the next meal. If he notices, that's not the fight he wants to fight. I don't find a space in the quiet to describe to him what happened below the 95 bridge. I pull away in my own secret place. This is new, our having secret places. I shut my eyes in the firelight, and I don't have to see his shoulders. My father says he's going out fishing at four a.m. Needs some sleep. "I'll drive all night," he says. He is still tall, filling the frame of the door to his room.

"Me, too," I say, letting Springsteen talk for us. It's a song about loving somebody so much you'd drive all night to bring them nothing but shoes, if shoes is what they want.

Alone by the fire, I remember last night, knowing now that Luke had been my father's deckhand. I remember the message my father left on the phone when the snow started.

I try to imagine the night of the storm for someone home

from a war. The soldier's eyes said he didn't sleep. It had started to snow at dinnertime and did not stop.

My father had called him and the phone rang and rang, maybe six or seven rings.

Maybe Luke stood in the dark, not answering. Maybe the snow flew into his windows like it did at our house, at right angles into the glass.

He would have listened to my father's message, "Sleep in. We'll wait out the storm."

WORLD CIV

Someone on snowshoes had made a path through the woods. The sea smell of low tide washes over me at the river. The rocks appear large on the beach, exposed by the tide. What if the soldier might jump down the rocky bank to the beach? I breathe in very slowly. Would he appear? Pilot scrambles across the stones, chasing a gull. I think of the dog's owner in a book I once read, *Cracker.* A soldier trained a dog to detect land mines in Vietnam. Once they even went on a rescue mission to Cambodia. I try to imagine the soldier and his dog—if they took a wrong step, the world could end.

The soldier doesn't come, not before I have to run back up the bank and through the white woods to go to school.

At 7:30 a.m., Mr. Murray will be at his desk. He's like a clock, and I like school with the steadiness of Mr. Murray. When Mr. Murray walks in, we settle in for the ride. World Civilization. He sits at his desk beside the blowup of a documentary photo my cross-country friend Daniel took. It's a tug, nearly fogbound, guiding a tanker in the dogleg of the Piscataqua River. On the facing wall is a map of the world as wide as the room without any borders to the countries, just rivers and mountains. Mr. Murray wears a blue shirt, white sneakers, khakis, and sturdy red suspenders with double hook straps. He glances up at the class almost sheepishly, his mouth lost in his white beard.

I almost laugh. He doesn't even know Rosa and I are taking him to the civilization of Chincoteague for the spring while my father wrestles the wolf and we eat BBQ at the Motel 6.

But my mind snaps back to the cold of the beam I might have walked on, balanced over the fast, outgoing water. The bridge, the blue-black river. The snow. The soldier.

"Would you join us, Miss Grear?" Mr. Murray says.

I look up, startled. I want to get him his coat right now and say hey, Mr. Murray, we're out of here. We're getting away from my mother and whatever fire is about to catch over the soldier—he is trouble and you know it—and head down to Chincoteague. With Rosa we'll howl and sing all the way, 533.4 miles by road my father says. But then I look out our window and think, Jesus, would the moon come, too?

I remember being on the edge of sleep as a little, little child riding with my mother in a car and seeing the moon keep pace, and hearing my mother singing, light and beautiful, about the rabbit in the moon.

I make myself sit in my hard desk chair and glance at Daniel, the photographer, and Taylor, whose black hair is teal blue today, and Binny, whose sister waits tables at the Friendly Toast. Mr. Murray hooks his thumbs under his suspenders and guides us back into the last century where I do not want to go.

HOLDING ON

After school on Friday, I wait down at the co-op for my father to steam in. I wait until the sun is bright pink and just threatening to sink beneath the end of the water. That's when I see the *Karma* come around the tip of Four-Tree Island. She's a steel-hulled boat, a shrimp dragging net rolled up on the steel spool at her stern, her name in red on her black-painted hull. I watch her slow progress through a white mist. On the boat, my father seems like a god. Is Luke his crew today?

I watch till my father hurls up the line to tie up. I swallow my pride to meet him like I used to meet him in the old days, the day before yesterday. He leaps onto the pier. Despite the tension between us, I feel the rush of relief when he wraps his arms around me. The cold from his body crosses into mine. But I look past him to the crewman still on board.

"Mighty cold night for you," he says, but he sees me looking on board, turns away, shakes his head. The crewman's face is buried in a hoodie and slicker. But I already know it's our old friend, Pete. "We got some work to do," he says. Pete is hosing down the deck. The driver is here to drive the totes of shrimp to Gloucester. They work fast. Pete's hands work with a rhythm. He hooks each tote on the winch, the crane lifts, the green box swings and rises to the pier.

The pink sun descends. For a while it hangs between the towers of the lift bridge that spans the river, the bridge nearest the co-op and the opening to the sea.

"Count 'em, thirty-four totes," my father calls up from the boat. I will write the number in the book at home. Thirty-four. A good enough trip.

"Can we go soon? Got work tonight," I say. I think of forlorn Vincent, my manager at Dunkin' Donuts. He hates me being late. I always am.

My father says he'll drive us home, then come back to finish up. The wind cuts through me, and the sun descends without a trace into the river. I leap into the truck that's weighted with lines and buoys and thick with the smell of fish and gear. I love the smell. I miss my father and want us back. The way we were without a mother.

"Dad, you don't have to go to Chincoteague. We'll have more good days."

I don't say my mother and grandmother won't have to move into our house.

He says, "Shrimping's almost done, and it just got started. I'm going."

We clank round the turns in the rattly truck that might be colder inside than the bare outdoors. He downshifts, and the snowy night muffles the truck's complaining screams. At our house the stack of traps spills over the driveway. The truck's headlights catch the blue dinghy.

"Dad," I say, "why don't we sell some of this at the winter market? Sell it ourselves."

"Can't," he says. "Don't have a permit."

"We'd get more money. We could make a lot with thirty-four totes."

"Like the way you think, boss. Maybe next year," he says, then lets it drop.

His mind is someplace else. And I also think of the phone

number at Kilim.

Atlantic Co. Local Broker. Good Prices.

We begin to unload the truck, and we stash a bucket of shrimp in a bin with ice. My father holds some back to give away or stock up in the freezer. "What if I take some to Atlantic? See what kind of deal we can get there?"

He shrugs. "Never saw them to support local fishermen. But you're the boss."

The moon plays through the trunks of the trees. I race to open the door, and Pilot flies into the snow dust. That's when I see my mother's yellow Corolla slide up in front of our house.

YOU THE DAUGHTER

In winter I have seen my grandmother grow orange peppers in her bedroom, saving the seeds for next year's garden. I saw it when my father and I visited my mother one Christmas. He had said, "Come on, it's Christmas. You need to see her."

I'd sat slumped in my mother's room, one that she rented with two other girls, all of them housekeepers at the Ashworth By the Sea near the strip at Hampton Beach. My grandmother slept there, too.

I was nine and sullen and dressed like a boy. That's what my grandmother said. I only remember I loved racing down to the river, filling bait bags with herring if my dad was hauling traps, stretching belly-down on the pier, calling out to the seals. How else was a kid going to dress?

That day, I was supposed to be at Rosa's, decorating little wreaths and reindeer cookies with sweet sugar glitter. Instead, I kept my distance from my grandmother, with her mean little eyes and sharp sour smells of cooking. My mother sprawled in a chair, her arms dangling over the sides. "Maid," she said. "I never worked so hard in my life. You don't finish a room in thirty minutes, they say you aren't working." Her eyes scrunch up. "Oh, my legs ache." My grandmother wasn't listening. She was yelling at my mother, and I understood that she wanted my mother to go with her to Lowell, to their old apartment.

"These Cambodian girls in America," my mother and grandmother had said. "They grow like giants." They were looking at me, mussing my T-shirt, my baseball cap. My grandmother talked in English that didn't match, and sometimes she didn't bother with verbs. Mostly I remember my grandmother demanding, "You come. You the daughter." I took my father's big, calloused hand to ward her off, terrified that she could make me. I would not take the cup of sticky rice that she tried to jam in my chest. But my father took it, and under his stern eyes, I ate.

I could already stitch bait bags as fast as a bufflehead could dive for food, and I could mend my father's nets. I was a fisherman's daughter from Portsmouth, New Hampshire. Nothing to do with these people.

But against my will, all the time I missed the smell of the room where I wouldn't talk to my mother. I felt her hand smoothing my shirt. I remember the surprising sweetness of the rice. I wanted her to have more than a room. I didn't want her legs to ache. Now and then she called me after she went with her mother to Lowell. What could I say? Please, please let me live with you in your room. I won't bother you.

I thought by sixteen, I'd be over her.

WHEN I SEE MY MOTHER

"I'm late," I call in that flash of a second before my mother's yellow car actually comes to a full stop in front of our house. "Taking the truck, Dad. Bye. Back around nine." I force Pilot in the house, nearly dragging her. "Go go go, you have to go!" She doesn't understand and cries. I shut her in anyway. I need to disappear in my father's truck.

But I can't stop myself from turning to look. Just at that moment, my mother steps out of her car and looks over her shoulder.

Her long black hair is lit by a yellow halo from the streetlight. My mother and I both slip our hands in our front coat pockets against the cold.

A sharp pain jolts me over the next thing I see.

She wears a white nylon puffy coat. It hangs wide open even in this cold, the two ends of the belt dangling. Silver buttons glint in the light, framing her belly, which the warm coat can't cover. Her belly bulges with baby.

I think two things at the same second. *How could someone like you be my mother?* And *A baby! How dare you?*

Even though I know it's that guy in Lowell she goes back to, I am betrayed, and she's never been mine. I am also pulled back to a house, a room, the pungent smell of lime and garlic in fish sauce, women chopping lemongrass, stringy strands of lemongrass, long windows swollen shut by ice and an overheated, suffocating Massachusetts night.

Women squatting, balling mounds of sticky rice for children who tear past them, laughing. I wear a tiara. I remember someone's hands placing the tiara in my hair.

It is my birthday party.

This is my own memory, coming loud as a freight train. I know the rhythm of the women's voices. The words in Khmer soften at the edges and turn to smoke. This can't be *my* memory. But the tiara is as real as my ring with the tiger's eye that Luke found. I swear I can feel the tiara on my head.

"Stay a while," my father calls. It stops me as I haul the truck door open.

"No."

My fingers touch the soldier's dog tags that nest in my pocket.

When I see my mother with a new unborn child I become a child. Did she put the tiara on my head when she was only a few years older than I am now?

I step up into the old Chevy with the "Save the Fishermen" bumper sticker on the back. My father follows me, his long legs slow and easy-does-it, even in the cold. He has something to say. I lower the window. "Dad, I need to go. Please." My voice rises. My mother is walking toward us.

"I told that kid I owe him one trip. When I let him go." My father doesn't look at me. "Said I'd take him on one more trip. Then he needed to find a new boat. He's a brawler in town, but on board, he never missed a beat. I allowed myself to shut my eyes when he was on board. The only crew I can say that for. You'll never see him again, Sofie."

I knew this was a command. The first I have ever heard from my father.

I pull out onto the street just in time.

STRIP MALL

"Late," Vincent says when I push open the door, clutching my apron and cap.

My boss never misses the time. I check the clock. It's five minutes after five. It could be much worse. I stash my coat, wrap my hair around my hand and pull it into a ponytail, put on the cap. Clock in. Tie on apron.

Vincent is built low and gorilla-like. He is gruff, tattoos bursting down his arms. If customers ask, he tells them about his tattoos. He designed them himself with symbols from all the cultures he is made up of. A koi fish on his bicep for the Japanese blood, a Celtic cross for the Irish blood, a muskrat he read about in a legend for his Abenaki blood.

"Forgive you this time, babe."

"Don't call me that, Vincent. I won't be late again."

"Don't be shy about it. You're not a California babe. But you're a babe."

Jesus, he irritates me so. If it weren't for the pay.

The Dunkin' Donuts is in a tiny strip mall with an Asian market that I've never been in. Behind it are the city's only projects, though hardly projects compared to the ones in Lowell and other cities in the Valley. The Valley is south of us, Lowell and Lawrence on the Merrimack River's banks where European immigrants came for jobs in the mills. Next the Hispanics and the Asians came, like my mother. Like me?

"Hi, what can I get for you?" I ask the customer at the drive-through who is only a voice in my ear. She lists a string of drinks and a dozen chocolate frosted. I fill the box of donuts. Pour the coffees with creams and skim and sugars. Get them to the window. This will continue for hours.

My hair is falling from my cap, and I jam it back under. The cap is beige with a tiny strip of orange around the bill and a cherry-red, orange, and white DD on the brim. I hate the cap. Vincent wears one just like it, plastering his thin hair to his head. He wears it low over eyes that are heartsick like a basset hound's. I imagine a story of unrequited love that left his eyes so bereft.

A girl comes in, her elbow loose around a guy's neck and him in jeans hanging beneath his hipbones. The girl wears earrings that dangle and long hair in spirals down to the small of her back. I know this couple likes their coffee with double milk, double sugar.

A tiny woman with pixie hair under a pink beret stares at the trays of donuts.

"Hi, what can I get for you?"

She comes every night. She's waiting for the time we throw out the donuts that have been on the rack too long. "May I have one of the cream filled?" she asks, very upper class.

"I'm sorry, that's against the rules," I say.

We each say this every night. And every night when Vincent's back is turned I put two cream filled in a paper bag for her. Vincent knows I do this.

Mrs. Bennett goes out with her donuts, easing her way up the sidewalk and through the crush of lights at the intersection of roads to the mall. I brew more decaf. Sometimes people want that at night. When I turn I see Mrs. Tuttle, who wears sequin ducks on her sweatshirt jacket, lean her head in the door. She's a neighbor from the Heights.

"I know your dad's a fisherman," she says. "Do you have any

Maine shrimp? I wonder if you'd sell me some shrimp straight from the boat. It's my husband's birthday. He is eighty-three tomorrow." Wind blows her most of the way inside. "I remember when they used to sell shrimp off a truck right here on Woodbury."

She means northern shrimp, what the New Hampshire fishermen call them. Tiny, sweet shrimp only in these northern waters. And that's when it comes together for me.

Brilliant.

"I can get you some shrimp for Mr. Tuttle's birthday," I say. "Whole shrimp?"

"I don't mind. Grew up cleaning shrimp. Ned Dickerson's got a thing going off his boat," Mrs. Tuttle says, "Whole shrimp. One seventy-five a pound."

"I can beat that," I say. "One seventy."

"Dickerson's getting a better price selling locally. It's a lot of work. Like they're giving out recipes and telling people how fresh tastes better than frozen." This conversation is happening around the orders coming in through my earpiece.

My head spins with possibilities for profit. And keeping my father home. He gets seventy-five cents a pound for the shrimp going to Gloucester. You don't have to be good at math to figure out it'd be good to sell to Mrs. Tuttle.

"Couldn't do it," Vincent says. He was doing a crossword between jobs back behind the counter. It's all filled in, in ink, with the tiny black letters, except for one tiny block.

"What's the question?"

He puts the clipboard away, slides the pen in the metal clip, and shakes his head. "Got standards," he says. I know the standards. 1: No reference, not even Sofie. 2: No guessing. 3: In ink. Vincent should be running a country, not a donut shop.

I mop, imagining measuring out shrimp for Mr. Tuttle's birthday. Wash out the pots. Put on my sweater, over the shirt that says *DD Oven Roasted, Gets You Running.* The floor shines. The traffic has grown lighter outside. The ribbon of lights that crosses the storefront has slowed. "'Night, Vince." I don't look back. "Five sharp tomorrow," he says in his way, and I don't have to look to see his heartbroken eyes.

Sometimes I wonder if it's Vincent who wrote on the seawall at the beach in all-cap black letters, *You were too beautiful for this world . . .*

When I step out, I instantly see him. The soldier is a silhouette, his boot on the runner of my father's truck, knee bent. I realize later that the command my father gave never crosses my mind.

THE ASHWORTH

The fear is the first thing. Of the rawness of him. Of his eyes, acutely on guard and tender at the same time. He watches me come. When I'm closer, I see the line of his lips. He takes me in, my eyes, my cheekbones, my hair.

I stop. I slowly slide the Dunkin' Donuts cap off my hair. His eyes soften.

Something almost like a smile crinkles in his eyes. We are not in color, like we were when the sun splashed in the sky. We are gray beneath hooded streetlights with streaks of white headlights cutting through us.

I start to shiver.

First my teeth. Then my shoulders and knees. At home, maybe my mother is still talking to my father. With her big belly. With that new baby. I see her more clearly than if I'd stayed at home. I can't picture my mother with me and Dad at the Formica table, fretting over the piles of papers—bills for fuel, bait, the new GPS, crew, boat mortgage, taxes, fish brokers, federal permits, documents for days at sea, what it cost one time Pete rammed the *Karma* over a rock in the channel.

Luke and I stand with our arms crossed against the cold. The sky allows haze from the moon to seep through. The moon is waning but bright.

"You're cold," Luke says, beside my father's truck.

"I'm scared," I say.

"Of me?"

I shake my head.

"Should I go?"

"Jesus," I whisper. "You better stay."

Then a laugh, a roaring laugh. We are nothing like we were on the beach in the snow and splotchy sunrise, when I was in shock over the gun and then lost with him. He is laughing. "Aren't you your father's daughter. *Jesus*. On the boat it's like he's calling up the spirits."

I smile. My father's daughter. Luke drops his boot to the ground. We face each other. He is laughing, but his hand shakes until he rests it low, on his thigh.

"Come on," he says.

Yes, I think. "Where?"

"Get some food."

It seems natural to go. I've been waiting for this. We get in his car. The seat cracks with cold, and I wonder how long he'd been standing with his boot on my runner. We drive out of the streetlights of the city, heading east. We pass the cemetery and follow out the dark roads and I know where these roads are leading, toward the ocean. We follow along the road that hugs the ocean in the winter dark and can hear the waves beat on the rocks as the tide crashes in. We are silent. It's late, and we've come so far, but my father will be asleep and when we come to Hampton Beach, I feel like I am the only place I could possibly be tonight. I know the beach, the strip. Rosa and I have come here all our lives to the shops and arcade along the boardwalk.

Luke pulls into one of the diagonal parking slots. I take him in as we walk. He's wearing a jacket that swings open over a thick, navy blue sweater, a baseball cap. He gives me a crooked smile as we walk along the strip. That's what they call the stretch of Ocean Boulevard with the boardwalk and Blinks Fry Dough, the casino, bead shops with shells and stones from all the wide world, Jerri's Breakfast, Ice Cream, Subs. Toe rings. On Memorial Day, in the crush of people, the police start patrolling. Break up the rowdies. Track the walkaways and reunite them with their moms.

"No place open," I say.

"One place. Ways to go. I just like walking the strip."

We keep walking. It's natural. Like we do this. I have school, Mrs. Bennett's cream filled, then race down the boardwalk with the soldier. We come to the arcade where you can put a quarter in to get the mannequin fortune teller to turn her gray head and spit out your fortune on a card, arcade games, shooting gallery, bowling lanes.

The arcade is closed. Light snow falls against the shuttered wall.

"I want you to listen and listen tight," I imitate the words that play on a loop in the shooting gallery. "I want you to shoot it and shoot it right," I recite. "It's the gunfighter in the shooting gallery."

"First weapon I fired when I was a kid. My friends and I used to come up from Nashua," Luke says. "I always went for the piano player."

"And the piano plays jive."

Then we list all the animated creatures in the shooting gallery and the sounds they make when you shoot them with laser guns on their small triangle targets.

"The bear . . ."

"Growls," I say.

"The clown . . ."

"His nose flashes."

I am laughing.

It's okay. He is okay about the bridge. And the pier. And the gun. He is okay talking about a shooting gallery everybody in the Merrimack Valley and everybody from the Seacoast over generations—the Italians, the Scots, even the Cambodians, everybody—knows. It's our history.

Luke knocks his cap down half over his eyes. "Where the hell did you come from?" he teases.

We cross the streets, D Street, C Street, B. "I walk the strip a lot," he says. We come to the Ashworth By the Sea. My father and I don't come here. But I know this is where we visited that Christmas years ago, a motel room on a side street that my mother rented. I know that some fishermen's kids work here as waiters and dishwashers in season. Luke opens the door.

"Food here?" I say.

We enter a dimly lit dining room with white lights strung across the ceiling like stars. We have entered a universe. I glance at this guy I am with, then around the Ashworth overlooking the seawall and the ocean. It's a dream to come here with him to eat dinner, two people who are very nearly strangers, but I can't remember not knowing him.

We have our pick of tables since the only other people here are zipping their parkas and paying their bill. We sit at a window table where we hear the waves crash on the seawall. I take off my coat. Then I take off my Dunkin' Donuts apron. I stuff it inside my coat to hide the scent of sugar and chocolate and coffee, but the smell is in my hair. Luke drops his cap on the table. Then he folds it and puts it in his pocket. I see his hands shake on the table. His eyes are green, wary, and bloodshot. His hair is dark. He plants his palms on the table. I think this is to steady them. We scan the menu and order fish and chips from the waiter.

He gives me his crooked grin. "Found you," he says.

"Maybe 'cause you gave me this," I say and slide his dog tags from my pocket. He glances at them.

"I wanted to set your mind at ease," he begins.

"I'm at ease." Like a challenge.

I look at him through my hair that I know is blown wild.

He shrugs.

"You mean about the gun," I say with an airiness I don't feel. "I've seen guns. This is New Hampshire." I laugh at my joke about a state where people come across the border to buy any kind of gun, rifle, handgun, AK-47.

I pull my hair back off my face and glance at him. He shrugs. It occurs to me there's no room with him to be fake.

"Maybe it's my mind I'm worried about," he says. "I'll quit obsessing over yours."

His eyes shift to the door, to the waiter bearing water. We hear the click of saltshakers that a busboy gathers on a tray. Is it like the click of a weapon when it's engaged? We're not going to talk about what he was doing with the gun. The question just sits on the table, a little groggy, while we watch each other and glance away, trying to pretend we're not.

The waiter is vacuuming. We are the only customers. Snow has begun to fall harder over the boulevard and into the sea. The food comes, and we dig in, famished.

"This place haunted?" Luke says, shifting his eyes to a dark hallway where the waiter turned off the lights.

"Oh, probably." I press my palms to my head, laughing. "Maybe it's the statue of the lady across the boulevard. It says, 'Breathe soft ye winds.' She's asking the waves to be gentle to sailors who died at sea."

He eats fast. He's cleaning up. He motions, *eat*, *eat*, at me and my plate that brims with golden fries. He eats, and I begin to tell him things. I tell him my mom is moving in.

"Heard a few things about that," he says, and I think of the long hours my father and he had on the boat. Did they talk about me?

I say, "She was sixteen when she had me. I hardly see her. When I was little I told my teacher she was a selchie, a seal woman, and she'd gone back to live in the ocean. Dad had to go and talk to the teacher."

Luke hoots. "A seal woman?" He lifts his chin, downing a beer. I smell the beer. I smell some scent, maybe the wool of his sweater. Some smell that is him. "You said she became a seal?"

So I tell him the Scottish tale about the carpenter who fell in love with a woman and they had a child. But she was also a seal, and when she found her sealskin, she swam back to her seal family in the ocean.

Luke leans in toward me, his head on his fists. His green, bleary eyes are staring at me like I've got something mysterious he could use. I can't turn my eyes from his. He says, "I'd like to try on a sealskin. Get out of this skin."

Then I pull back. We both do. He calls for another beer. I hug my coat around myself, chilled beside the black windowpane. I say, "Since this threat of seeing my mother, I keep having these flashbacks about her."

His eyes narrow, like I've become dangerous. "Did something happen you can't let go of?"

"Just moments. Just smells. What about you?" I say. "I want some secrets, too."

He downs half the new glass of beer. He says, "Zurmat. Paktia Province."

I know these names. Afghanistan.

"So you're back, you're not going."

He nods. "I think about going back, all the time."

"What did you do?" I say.

A tiny squinting of his eyes. He had shaved. But I can see a shadow in the valley over his lips. "Medic," he says. "Cordon and search missions."

I don't know what that is. "I've seen photos of Afghanistan," I say. I place myself in a classroom with Mr. Murray showing photos on the screen. "Mountains and valleys," I say. "They need to irrigate the little farms."

His eyes shift to mine. "You're so pure."

I don't know what to say. I just nod. Then, "I need to go."

"I know," he says.

"Where do you live?" I say.

"Near Rye Harbor. A winter rental. One of those cabins.

That's why I got this habit now of coming down here and walking the strip. Not much life, but enough."

"My father lived in one of those winter rentals. It had everything. Near Rye Harbor? The ones in a horseshoe by the stone ledge?"

"Yeah," he says. "It's fine."

It's not.

I can tell from his face. He doesn't want to go back to it. I'm not pure. I feel like I'm old, like the way I felt when he took off his sunglasses and dared me to look at him on the beach.

"Wanted to say thanks." He is standing.

"For what?"

"Bad night, that night. Thanks for stopping. You could have run for your life."

I stand to go, too, even while I'm pretending we are going back to his cottage, in the center of the horseshoe of cottages. From there it's a short walk to a stone breakwater reaching out to the Isles of Shoals.

His phone beeps.

He zips his coat over his sweater and answers.

"Yup," he says. "No problem." Puts the phone in his pocket.

"Don't tell my father," I say.

"Tell him what?" Luke says. He's distracted. He doesn't look at me.

"That we're doing this. He thinks I'm perfect, that if he warned me, I would never do this."

At the door, he looks at me. Straight on. We are so close I imagine the hardness of his jaw under the shadow of beard.

"We're not doing anything," he says. He shoves his hands in his pockets when we step into the wind.

"Why do you say it that way?" I ask.

"I don't want to get used to you," he says. His jaw has hardened, and he moves ahead of me. He had not hesitated. But I know why he's trying to put dark and space between us. I can name a dozen reasons why we should not get used to each other.

I catch up but let it be. We walk across the boulevard, our chests and hair quickly layered in snow. I am aware of his body and my body. He is barely two inches taller. Something happens to my walk. I feel it in my toes and my heels as my boots make silent prints beside his. I feel every part of them, making an arc as I am simply walking.

I'm already used to him.

FLYING

I get home at midnight from Dunkin' Donuts and the Ashworth By the Sea where I ate dinner and smelled beer I never drank. My father is asleep. The sky must be clearing, and my father will go fishing in the morning. I am flying, simply remembering Luke's eyes. Remembering when I first saw his boot on my truck's runner, the bend of his leg, the charge through my body.

I make a cup of coffee with hot milk. I see Luke's crooked smile and his dark hair that falls across his forehead.

My father snores himself awake. Then he's quiet. I will sell our shrimp. Fresh-caught sweet northern shrimp to make us rich.

The house is still. The roar of traffic over the bridge has not stopped, but it has let up enough so outside there are seconds of absolute quiet. I have a memory of the sound of a helicopter's rotors over the river the night my father and I worked on the shrimp nets. A witness must have seen someone stop his car, get out. I feel relieved tonight there are only the normal sounds of traffic, steady, people maybe going home.

While I pack my father's lunch for him to take fishing, somehow I also think of the map of old Afghanistan Mr. Murray showed us, where traders made paths through the mountains as they crossed between continents.

In a few hours my father will be up and brewing coffee at three thirty. He'll take the sandwiches I'm making. I'll hear the truck start, and he'll have food and hot coffee in a thermos as he steams off shore. And Luke will be on board.

GHOSTS

I wake in the morning. I remember the small valley above Luke's lips under the shadow of beard. It's mysterious how his eyes draw me. It's as if we each know something the other wants to learn.

But when I come down the stairs, half asleep, I stop still on the landing. A figure steps onto the porch beside my father's traps. Long dark hair down her back. I hadn't heard the car. Pilot did not warn me. Pilot stands, curious. What now? She is my mother. She has seen me through the window, and I can't pretend I'm not here. When she knocks, I stare. Then go to the door and allow her in.

My mother's cheeks are thin while her belly is large. She pulls her hair up and folds it into itself at the back of her neck. She gives me her wide smile. "Sophea." She says my Cambodian name, pronounced *so-PEE-ya*. Although no one calls me that, it doesn't sound unfamiliar. I sit down in a chair, rigid, drawing my knees up and protecting my chest. "Why are you here?" I say.

She looks like an exhausted teenaged girl who somehow got herself pregnant.

She smiles. Sheds her puffy white coat. She sits on the couch and watches me for a brief second.

"I don't feel good," she says. "Is Johnny here?"

I don't like it. She has no right to need my father.

She leans her body forward, lowers her head, and a small moan escapes.

"He's fishing," I say.

"I might be sick," she says.

Just in time I grab the big blue bowl my father and I use for lobster claws. My mother leans over and retches, and my thought, from nowhere, is that it feels tragic to see her loss of dignity. She is so perfectly made, her hair in waves, her blush, her straight spine, her English. She retches loudly, and tears fill her eyes. I turn around in my long johns till the sounds stop.

Under her coat she's wearing velvety pants and a white shirt, and without her boots, she's barefoot. Loose hair falls over her face. Slowly, she eases it back and takes the bowl into the bathroom.

"Mom," I say when she returns. I don't say her retching is making me queasy. "I'm getting ginger ale. That's what my father gives me when I'm sick." I jam my arms in the sleeves of his old coat. "Back soon," I sing. But I could let the tide rise and fall and rise again before I come back, and my mother will not drink the ginger ale. She will put a leaf on her tongue. A Cambodian remedy. I'd have more luck if I got her a plant.

My mother is quiet. Her head remains lowered over the bowl. Any human person would rest their hand on the tight tendons I see in the back of her neck to comfort her. I can't.

I am standing behind her, and she reaches her slender fingers over her head to touch me. This hurts me so badly. Like the wind, it will stop. Disappear. I see bracelets made of glass beads on her wrist. I know that she has eyeliner tattooed above her lashes. When she looks up it won't be smeared, in spite of the tears that have sprung up with her sickness.

"Ginger ale's the ticket," I whisper. I open the door. A blast of snow flies in.

I hear her say, "I don't need ginger ale. I'm pregnant. Ginger ale will not make me stop throwing up." She leans over the lobster bowl, then stretches herself out, the length of the couch. Her bare, red-painted toes show at the hem of her trousers. I see her skin is nearly as brown as the wood of the armrest. I don't think I had ever noticed.

"I know," I say.

"What do you know? Wait till you're pregnant."

"I will never get pregnant." I am sure of this.

"I will never get pregnant," she repeats. Is she mimicking me? She throws her arms up, and her bracelets fall down her wrists and tinkle.

"How could you let yourself get pregnant?" I am standing over her, my arms are in the air. I am both ashamed and excited I might know where I could find my father's bottle of gin because when my mother is gone I will take a small taste and let my head spin like a dream.

"I don't know," she says. "We were little kids in the camps. Bong Proh and me. He's too old. I won't go back to him."

"I don't want to know about your personal life."

"It could happen. You aren't perfect," she says.

She goes right to my gut. I say, "I have to go to work." I glance at her eyes that I know are exactly like mine.

"How long since you came to see me?" my mother says. But she doesn't listen. She stands. Beneath her unbuttoned shirt is a cami, stretched wide across her belly. She tenderly, slowly bends to lift a scarf from her back and tie it around her neck, slides her bare feet into boots. Even her toes, which must be so cold on the wood floor, somehow enrage me. She pulls her large, quilted jacket over the scarf. "Could you give me a ride?" she says. "I have a doctor's appointment. They'll check the heartbeat. I think something is the matter. I've been sick every morning, and I'm already seven and a half months. I have very bad karma." She ends in a soft whisper.

"Why does the world revolve around you?" I say.

"Oh, it's okay," she says. "I'll find a way." Perfectly applied to shift the blame to me. Watch your mother with morning sickness turn and walk out the door. Seven and a half months.

"I don't have a car." I am both seething and helpless.

She takes me in, measuring me. She doesn't ask, *How would you go to work?*

"I do," she says. "But they took my license. Please drive."

I do not ask what she did to lose her license or why she would drive to my house and not to the doctor. I imagine the archived tickets in her gold-lacquered vase, the driving without registration, insurance, license, glasses, Johnny to help her.

My mother and I sit at opposite ends of the doctor's office waiting room. My mother is a snow queen in her white jacket, hood up, fake fur around her eyes.

Her eyes are black and wide with fear. Are mine? I move a couple chairs closer.

"What's the matter, Mom?"

Her dark eyes flash to mine, almost as if she is embarrassed to show this side of herself to me. "There's a ghost in me."

"What do you mean?"

"It's true. You can feel it."

She holds out her hand to me. I can't bear it. I move to the seat beside her.

She takes my hand. She holds it to her belly under the white jacket. I am wearing finger gloves. I lift my naked fingertips. Only my protected palm feels the jump, of feet? Of a butt?

"Sometimes at night I hear the ghost singing," she whispers.

I pull my hand back. I pick up *New Hampshire Home* from the stack of magazines.

I open to a house on the Piscataqua, a long porch with a view of the river, an elegant table set for dinner with goblets, and with napkins folded like birds.

"It's true," my mother says. "I remember the singing of ghosts. I heard it in the camp when I was a tiny girl."

In the picture in *New Hampshire Home*, a single green rocker faces the water. I am there. I pretend Luke and I pull up to the dock by the porch in the boat, and we are sprayed with water and laughing.

"They are the ghosts of the people that died. They take you over. Do you remember when we lived in Lowell?"

I feel like I'm looking into a mirror. Who's that girl? I remember my sparkly tiara.

"But the ghost crept into me there," my mother tells me.

"It wasn't a ghost. Dad said you couldn't take care of me."

My chest. There is a monster. It is squeezing my chest between its hands and taking my breath. I drop the magazine on the stack.

"I'm opening a fresh-off-the-boat shrimp stand. I'll make good profit. So, Mom, maybe he doesn't need to go to Chincoteague."

Her scared black eyes meet mine. Does she know what this means? That she can't move in. She and the ghost.

The nurse calls, "Lydia Sun."

It's my heartbeat you should check, I think. *Something is the matter with my heart.*

I don't have one.

I wonder if I have a ghost in me. If it can happen to my mother it can happen to me. I have her fear, like a little animal in me.

FEAR

My father had a good trip. A good day. We don't mention the soldier. But that night we let our guard down, exhausted, sitting by the woodstove in dim light. I'm on the couch, my father's in his wide-armed chair, the seat sunken to his weight, our long legs stretched forward, feet crossed at the ankles toward the stove, leaning back, our heads against our clasped hands. Pilot, asleep on my boot.

This is us. But we're also different. There's something butting in. I want to give it a shove into the open; I want to talk about it. I say to my dad, "What scares you?" I wonder if the Motel 6 in Chincoteague is creepy; I wonder if the expanse of ocean off Virginia has more ghosts than the Gulf of Maine. He thinks about my question.

"Well," he says. "Sometimes thinking about you scares the life out of me. When you were younger, you'd fall asleep, your hair would fall over your cheek. Just looking at your cheekbone scared me with how much I wished I could protect you."

We are silent. I think about begging him to take me to Chincoteague. Me, Rosa, and Mr. Murray. But I don't. I say my fear. "My fear is—trying to figure out how to say this. It's about your first wife."

"Who am I marrying next?" His exhausted eyes twinkle at me, and I love him.

"Don't know yet." The fire pops. "But the first one, she's a wild card, isn't she? We're doing good, you and me, and then here comes Lydia, and everybody starts to fight. Who needs this?"

My father doesn't answer that. I wonder if he knows about Bong Proh, the man too old for my mother, but someone from that war so they must be tight. The baby's father. The baby who comes walking into our lives curled inside my mother's belly.

In this deep scaredness inside me, there's Luke. I don't understand. I see his eyes bleary with no sleep, but they also warm me and hold me. So I make a fear up for Luke, one I don't tell my father.

What would Luke's fear be? Not the 95 bridge. Not the cars screaming. Not the speed of the current if a guy jumps. All these can ease a body. His fear is behind the eyes. It wedges his eyelids open. I imagine the clock ticking, the waves against the rocks, nothing he wouldn't do for sleep. His fear is that he can't go there. What do you do if you can't sleep? He needs to keep sorting the net as it flies through the winch and shave the snow from his nostrils and mouth the way I've seen my father do on the boat. And now he doesn't have a boat and that adds to his sleeplessness.

Pilot wakes and paces by the door, as if she feels tension in the house and she's worried we might leave.

SPANISH DANCER

Rosa holds out a white paper bag. "My mother made these." Inside are warm circles of pastry sprinkled with cinnamon. "*Pastelitos*," Rosa says.

We sit at the Formica table and eat, dusting our lips in confectioners' sugar.

"It's illegal," I say. "But we'll do it out of the garage. Word of mouth. You in?"

"What do you mean it's illegal?"

"Nothing's going to happen. It's a fisherman thing."

Rosa lifts her guitar and begins to strum.

"We're just selling shrimp, right?

"That's all we're doing. Just a hundred pounds. One tote."

"I don't see why you're doing it. If it's illegal."

"If I can sell for him—by myself, to see how it works—it will change our whole business model. We're not making it."

"Sofie, nobody's making it in the business. It's not your dad. It's the ocean."

I feel my lips grow taut like my father's when he's angry, even though I know she's right. Just last night Pete was talking about selling his quota of what the government allows him to catch to try to get out from under some of his debt.

"Forget it, Rosa. Just forget it, okay?"

Now Rosa tries to fix us. She says, "Okay, so my mom's a pastry cook. What do I know?"

I don't answer. I want to say, *You're right . . . you don't know anything.*

"I'm worried about you, Sofie. Don't you eat anymore? Look at you."

She reaches forward, runs her hands down my cheekbones. I put my face up to hers and trace my lips with my finger to show her the confectioners' sugar I can still taste.

"Who doesn't eat?" And she traces her lips with her finger and we stick out our tongues and we laugh. But it's true about how little I feel like eating.

"I'll do it," she says.

I say, "I have to fix the ocean. We need to make it here together, my father and me. Or he's leaving."

Rosa puts her guitar down and pulls up a song she's been learning on her phone.

"Hold off," Rosa says. "Fix the ocean later. Get your guitar."

"No, you play."

We listen to this melody while I begin to letter a sign for our illegal trade on the back of an old poster project.

Rosa plays along to the song on her guitar, "Spanish Dancer." It's a girl nervous about love, wondering what it was like for her mother, when she was young.

I pull up the chain of the dog tag that I now wear around my neck.

Sanna
Lucas
O negative
Protestant

Universal donor. His blood will match with anybody's. Even mine.

We wear half gloves with the red tips of our fingers working machine fast. We pack plastic bags with Mrs. Tuttle's shrimp. Put ten bags of shrimp over ice in an ice chest, with the sign mounted on poster board. *Sweet Northern Shrimp Fresh Off the* Karma.

We sit, our heads propped on our mittened hands, ready. Drivers do stop.

"How much would it cost for shrimp without heads, ready to cook?" a serious young woman asks.

"Six dollars a pound," I say, believing a person would never pay six dollars for a pound of shrimp.

"Atlantic asks seven," she says. "And I know your father. I'd rather have the *Karma*'s shrimp."

"Take these, and the next time you come, we'll have processed shrimp."

The woman finally does take the whole shrimp and pays three dollars for two pounds. We sell all the shrimp we have.

BREATHING IN THE BUDDHA

It's Sunday. My father's out fishing. It's today or maybe never. Could be only a few more landings till the government closes shrimp season. That's the rumor.

I lift a tote of shrimp I could have taken to Atlantic Co. I lift it up the porch steps, over the door sill, then slide it across the floor and into the kitchen. One batch at a time, I drop the shrimp in my pot of boiling water. One minute.

A car pulls up in the street. In the full light of day I see a maroon car, Luke's car, with the rust of New Hampshire winters eating into the fenders. He's not in camouflage; he's in jeans and a navy fisherman's sweater. He is coming toward my door. I rub my hands dry and watch him. His walk is deliberate. He turns to glance at a kid up the street, the neighbor's cat that streaks by.

He knocks. My hands are red and wet. Pilot is barking. I am wearing leggings and a ribbed shirt. My hair is up in a clip. My body's tender on the first day of my period.

I open the door.

Pilot leaps into his arms. She never forgets someone who has given her food. Luke comes down to his knees for her. I see Luke's bowed head of dark hair.

"My father's not here." I back up to keep from touching his hair.

"I need to talk to him," he says. "Find out when he's planning to fish."

"He is fishing."

"Did he say how long?" He looks up.

"Till supper. Maybe."

He lifts his hands from my dog's ears, slowly stands.

"Are you good at processing shrimp?" I say.

"Teach me."

Lines from Rosa's love song almost spill out of me. I cover my mouth to keep me from laughing and manage to open the door all the way without tripping on Pilot.

He comes in.

Has he ever seen a kitchen as small as this one? We work over the mound of shrimp in the kitchen sink, ready.

"Flip it over," I say. "Open the shell. Pull out the meat. It's a three-step process."

I glance at his face. The past is in his face. I see that he hasn't slept. He turns his exhausted eyes to me.

"Just be careful of these." I touch the long needle tail of the shrimp he is holding.

"You got to pop the head," I say. "Like this."

I hold a shrimp so he can see my finger slide down the line from the shrimp's head to the tip of the sharp tail. I twist the tail to expose the eatable flesh. Then pull the flesh out of the head and shell that encases it. I drop the curve of meat into the basin. I drop the crusty outside—eyes and all—into the trash bin.

Luke gets it in a heartbeat.

Open, twist, pull. We work.

I am aware of his hands. They are large and careful, manipulating something so small. There is something about what we are doing that feels sacred. An image of my grandmother comes into my brain. When I was little, I remember seeing her lift her hands, palms touching, and bowing to a fish. She said something in her strange, bad English. Something about giving respect.

The work with our hands—Luke's and mine—is as regular as breathing. I turn a shrimp in my hand. I begin to pull open the peel and a stream of water spews into my face and Luke's face.

"Ahh, it peed," I burst out laughing. "Ahhhhh." Luke wipes the wet from my face with the heel of his hand, holding the carapace in the other. I am laughing. Pilot yelps, waiting for a shrimp to drop.

"You must be a great cook," Luke says. "You're cooking for a banquet."

I don't say yes, I don't say no. I don't say it's illegal what I'm planning to do with these shrimp. I say, "I don't know what it is about you, but when I'm with you, I wonder what it would be like to be a Cambodian girl. Things about my mother's culture. Maybe because you're so different from my life. I've always been my father's girl."

"You're an enigmatic girl." He studies me. "Your mother who's coming. She's Cambodian?"

"She's crazy." I shrug. "She's not anything to me."

Pilot catches a shrimp and runs with a pink tail hanging from her mouth.

"Out," I yell at her. "Out."

I want to talk about the gun. Where's the gun? I hope you have gotten rid of the gun.

I remember a story. My grandmother and her friend sit together in the dusk. They talk in Khmer. When I was little I must have understood some Khmer. It's a story tucked deep inside me; it's hard to find and let into my head. I don't remember the story now, but I smell the hot peppers my grandmother was pressing with a mortar at dusk. Her story scared me so much—or maybe it was her own grief as she told the story—the smell of the peppers reminds me: be very afraid.

"One trip," Luke says, "I was banged up from an incident the night before. Had two black eyes. Reeked the hell of beer. Your dad must have thought he was taking on bad luck. Found a new guy."

I look over at the circle around his eye, close to the maroon color of his car. I want to touch his check. Suddenly a deep sadness takes me over, and I want to tell him to quit drinking his life away. And I barely know him. I can't stop this wave of sorrow that wants to take me over and I'm so scared it's not about him but it's about my mother 'cause I just met him. How can it be about him? I just want . . . I don't even know what I want. I want to go back to being my father and me.

"Look," I say. "Thanks. Thanks for helping." I wipe my hands on the checkered towel around my waist.

He pauses. I'm flaking on him, as Rosa would say. He knows it. My face must have closed down to him. "You want me to tell my father to give you a call?"

He looks at me like I kicked him in the gut. Shakes his head. "Keep him out of it," he says.

He's at the door, shoving his arms in his jacket sleeves.

"I'm sorry," I say. "My father told me you were the only crew he'd had on board he trusted enough for him to get some sleep."

He nods, his face stony.

I think of my father and Luke as both soldiers and being there for each other. But Luke is down the front steps.

I say, "He runs a tight boat." I don't say my father told me I'd never see him again.

My dog is blocking Luke's escape. She leaps and dances in his path as he tries to get to his car. She bows down in play between him and the car's door.

Already I'm second-guessing and plotting how I could see him again, even while he's trying to tell Pilot to get in, go home, to me. We won't see each other at school. We're not going to my spring dance in my high school gym with Daniel and the cross-country team. I'm not going to invite him here for my father's fried chicken and potatoes. I say finally, "Which cottage is yours?"

"Five," he says almost under his breath. Then looks at me one last time, shaking his head, like what the hell was he thinking?

Like, what do you expect meeting some high school girl under a bridge?

I sing Rosa's melody to myself slow as the setting sun, just the way I take in the last few drops of gin I find in the cupboard. My father never said don't drink. He should have. I simply ache, like the Spanish dancer in the song. I sit on the floor, letting the drops of gin burn my throat, and it feels like a shadow is beside me, a weight dragging me.

With this weight I go back to the bin of shrimp. Open, twist, pull. Discard the tiny carapace. Keep my father home.

MR. MURRAY'S FEAR

Mr. Murray continues to bring order to my morning. 7:30 a.m. He is always at his desk. We have regular assignments every week. I know if I am not there that day, he is, and he'll know I'm not there. Mr. Murray's and my days don't hinge on the wind in the birches or the government.

My head spins a little while I sit in his class Monday morning.

"You need to get in your assignments," he says before other students have come.

"Yes, I will."

"Before I'm gone."

"Are you going, too? Everybody's leaving."

"Who else is leaving?"

"My father's going fishing in Virginia."

"I'm only going to see my new grandson."

"When's that?"

"End of the week."

"I don't know," I say. "About getting the assignments in."

"Why not?" he says.

It was nice to stop thinking for a while, with the gin. I haven't done my assignments all week. I just look at him.

Mr. Murray gazes at me briefly, this man with vast curiosity about the world.

My father said that Mr. Murray's wife left him for a job in the city. She wanted more than he had to offer: a sweet smile, an appreciation for her walk, a good sentence. Mr. Murray writes a column for the newspaper. He never remarried, and my father said sometimes you can't account for who you fall in love with.

Later, during my study hall, I go to Mr. Murray's room and write one assignment. I think I might want to talk to him, but I don't. I just hang out there and work. Mr. Murray must wonder why I'm there.

I am still thinking about fear, after that night by the stove when my father and I talked.

Before I leave I drop a paper on his desk. It's a poem we read in English: "For My Young Friends Who Are Afraid."

I like it, quite a lot, but don't know how to use it right now, for my father and me. Maybe Mr. Murray will.

AT HIGH TIDE

I make a new sign. The last one got snowed on when Rosa and I sold the shrimp I cleaned Sunday.

> Sweet Northern Shrimp
> Fresh Caught
> $1.50/pound Whole
> $6.50/pound Cleaned Ready to Eat

I had cleaned a few more from yesterday's haul. I sell one last time while my father is fishing. Tomorrow I'll give him the money to prove this will work. We're okay.

Last thing before work, Pilot and I run down to my beach. I remember my father singing in his warbly voice as I run. I squeeze my eyes shut at the sun on the beach. I have this thought of me swimming in the sea like a seal. I pretend I can breathe under water and I can dive and glide through the waves. The idea takes my breath away since it is like dying to me—to go in the sea. The sun makes long shadows. My legs look like stilts as we run with the sun over my shoulder.

Vincent is melancholy tonight, more so than usual. He is silent as a large cat, galumphing up and down, picking donuts for customers. I ring them in at the register. Then fill the containers of sugar, skim, milk, cream.

"Where you from?" I say to try to shift the sullen mood of the place.

"Nowhere," he says, "Got some family in Salisbury."

"Nice beach," I say.

"Used to be," he says. "My grandmother used to go hear bands play in the oceanside joints." This seems to devastate him to tell it today, how the bands played, from the way his eyes droop.

I myself am euphoric! After I'm out of here, I'm driving myself to an oceanside joint. Rye Cottages. Number five. January has stretched long and cold, and now it's time.

My shift hangs on and on, the rhythm of the work taking on a life of its own. You're invisible unless you forget the three sugars. I get through it by singing. I pretend Rosa is here, and I sing.

I drive the dark roads toward the ocean and the horseshoe of cottages. I know where they are and take the left turn just past Rye Harbor, just past the breakwater that waves crash over at high tide. It is just high tide now. I drive around the curve of cabins. It is not hard to find number five.

He didn't invite me.

"Not a good idea," Luke says at the door. I feel the heat of the wood fire on my frozen cheeks.

I say, "I just got off work." As if that explains it.

He steps back from the door. He leaves a space, that's all. His step is loose, his shoulders seem like one is hitched up, one down. He is a little drunk.

"Last time I got off work, you were standing at my truck." I don't leave the door. I had changed my shirt in the bathroom at work and now stand with my boots feeling like they are pinned to the floor, my body off balance. "That's why I came."

His eyes focus on me for only a second. I can't read him. I glance around the room, unsure who he is.

Luke has nothing. A duffel. A beat-up phone on a charger by the bed. A book, maybe from the slim shelf of books for the rental. The book is in his hand. *On the Road.* He is preoccupied. I see a square of cardboard and a black pen, tubes of paint. He has been painting, but he moves the picture before I can see. I continue to look around the cottage. Chipped ivory crockery, so old it has veins, is stacked on open shelves. From the next cottage we hear a baby cry.

He lifts his hands to his hips. "You want coffee?" he says. He doesn't look at me, but gestures toward the kitchen, which is that shelf of plates, a stove, a small humming refrigerator.

I laugh. "I'm a coffee bean already."

Maybe against his will, he gives me his crooked smile. The black hair falls down his forehead.

"I've read Kerouac," I say. I stay by the door, but I feel my boots release from the floor and my body drawn into his room.

Luke pours himself a cup of coffee. It smells scarred and burned. The baby next door grows more unhappy. "Somebody crossed him," Luke says about the wails.

"We should get that kid a floppy-eared rabbit to play with."

Luke strides from the bed to the back door, facing the ocean, back and forth. I take in the dark and beyond, the ocean. He says, "Not sleeping. Can't remember when I slept. Hey, you hungry?"

Now he keeps talking.

"Not hungry," I say.

But he searches the cupboards. He finds tubs of peanut butter and leftover condiments from takeout dinners. "What do I have? Juice. Can't remember the kind." He finally pauses.

"Jeeze," he says. This word comes out in one long breath. "Sit down." Besides the bed there are kitchen chairs, a small drop-leaf table. I sit on one of the chairs. He spins a chair around, mounts it backwards, and sits facing me. "I'm going to look at you a while." He inhales, like he is breathing in my hair and my body. "Oh, Christ," he whispers.

The back of his chair is between us. I drop my arms. I take him in with my eyes.

I throw my head back. Exhale. Even the baby is silent for a beat.

"What are you doing here?" he whispers.

The answer is so simple. I don't hesitate to say it. "I want to be with you."

Then he's up, and he nearly throws the chair. "Your father won't even let me fish with him. Let alone . . ." I don't move. He says, "No. Besides. This place is for the walking dead."

I ignore this. "We can," I say. "I can come back here. We can hang out."

His face is distorted with pain.

"You're a kid," he blasts out, but it's as if he's blasting himself.

"I know a lot," I say.

"In Afghanistan they give girls like nine to old men."

"I'm seventeen in February. You're barely what, twenty?"

"Old man. Twenty-two," he says.

He lifts his head. "You should get out of here."

"My mother was sixteen."

"You told me," he says.

"My father. I am everything to him. I wish I weren't bad."

"You don't know what bad is. You're a child."

He comes down from his rage. He kneels. He places his hands on my shoulders. I close my eyes. I take in his smell of paint and beer and coffee and skin.

A charge runs through my body. His hands are warm and very big against the bones of my shoulders and back. "You must have dreams. What do you want to be?"

I laugh, opening my eyes. "I'm not six. Like, do you want to be a cowboy? I'm already it. I'm a businesswoman."

But Luke is back to pacing this space. He has lost interest. What can he say to a schoolgirl?

"What are you going to do now?" I say.

"What is this, the golden hour?"

"I don't know what that is."

"After a trauma, like an explosive in your chest, the first hour, the golden time when you have a chance to save somebody. Your only chance."

"No," I say.

I stand up in the tiny room that is kitchen, living room, bedroom. Where is the gun?

What I say is, "You need music in here."

"I don't speak the same language," he says.

"As who?"

"As any fuckin' person in this country. Move on, Sofie. Go out with the girlfriends. Or the boyfriends. You got a trail of them."

"We do," I say. "Speak the same language." I don't know why I know this. I lean against the counter, I hope provocatively. Luke steps away from me. He opens the cottage door. The footprints I left on the path when I came are covered with snow.

His outstretched arm grazes my shoulder. Rests.

"The family's trying to hook me up with this Odyssey project, some mountain at the end of the world. A vet thing. My family wants the guy I used to be back."

"Odyssey," I repeat.

He drops his arm. His face turns dark. But his eyes don't turn away. "The old guy's gone."

NO RETURN

The light is on. Not like my father. He never makes it this late. He crashes by eight or nine. But then he never leaves a room with a light on. What could we begin to have to talk about? Tell him, don't make me sneak any more shrimp? I'll just take it, okay, 'cause selling your shrimp is my last chance to keep you home.

When I see the light on, a part of me feels a reprieve and it's joyous. My father and me. We could go back to the way we used to be. Before all the things that have started spinning. For one brief second, I would be so happy to go back to just my father and me. And Luke? I don't know.

Snow blows into my jacket and chills my neck. I open the door.

"Where are you selling these?" Grim lines cut into my father's face.

"What, Dad?"

He hauls up a sign I'd made, *Sweet Northern Shrimp*.

"I sold every one," I tell him. "It was an experiment." I keep talking under his grim gaze, hoping it will turn when he understands. "I processed one of the totes. I wanted to see if I could sell them. I undercut Atlantic and sold them all."

"Where?" He is clipped.

"Right here. People really like it when it's processed."

"All you put in the ice chest?"

"I wanted to prove to you," I say again, as if that would explain everything. It is all for my father. Snow falls around us. I imagine the house disappearing. I wait for him to get it. Get how much money we'd made toward paying the bills.

"You said you were taking it over to Atlantic." My father shoves some papers on his desk. "I was letting you do it. Be the businesswoman."

"We can make a third more selling the shrimp ourselves. Atlantic wasn't offering much more than the wholesalers. They were robbing us. Don't you see?"

"Here's what I see." My father is stone-faced with rage. He cannot even look at me. "There's an ocean of paperwork behind selling. The law says you got to have a license to sell. You got to have a peddlers' permit. You got to get inspected. Got to get a state license. Got to get a federal license."

I feel my arms droop by my side as he blasts these words.

"The reason people don't do what you did is because the fine the government lays on you could be enough to shut a boat down."

"What do you mean?" He is too angry. He is enraged. He is red with fury. "Did they shut you down on account of what I did?"

"*You're* shut down. That's what I mean." He turns his rigid back and strides away, then bellows, "Get all that stuff out of here. They cited me, on account of what you did. They said, 'Grear, you got your daughter up to something on the side?' Do you know what they fine fishermen for illegal sales? Do you know there's not a breath a fisherman takes that doesn't have a law attached to it?"

I burst into tears.

"It was so you didn't have to go. I don't want you to go."

I run after my father. "Please don't go."

"Leave me alone, Sophea."

MY FATHER IS GOING

The next day, we get the news the government is shutting down shrimping early. They sent out a scientist to test the shrimp population. My father can tell you, scientists couldn't find a fish if there were a trail of gulls leading the way. Why don't they send fishermen who know where the fish are? That's what my father says.

Early in the morning, I hear him downstairs. He's on the phone, making plans to take the boat to Chincoteague. "Fine is going to set me back," I hear him say. "Seven hundred bucks. They're doing their best to rid the state of fishermen."

I shut my eyes. Seven hundred dollars! I slip down the wooden stairs, sit on the bottom step and listen. Pilot leans in. My father is at his computer, getting the marine forecast. It's one a.m.

"Dad, are you leaving?"

"Not today. Got things to do."

"Dad, please forgive me." I want to talk, but I am stupid with the wrongness of me. I am gulping down sobs. Between all the chokes and sobs, I say, "If it weren't for the shrimp you would stay. Let me come. I'll get all the assignments. I'll stay in the motel room. You'll never know I'm there. Dad, please." He won't be able to make out this last: "I've been so bad. I'm too young."

"How could you come? Since when you been on a boat? And your dog? What's your plan?"

I am bundled in sweats and a blanket. I drag our old rocker to my father's desk.

He pats my hand. Pilot shows the most concern. She does not like humans crying and tries to wriggle, long legs and all, into my lap. I sob. My father pats.

"I'll be back in May. Not so long."

"May!"

"Could be sooner. You'll get to know your mom."

"Jesus."

We sit in silence. Lydia Sun. Are we both thinking about Lydia Sun? It is all so bad. One thing after another. And then a *baby*. A baby long before May.

"Dad," I say, "how do you get good karma?"

He is hunched over the computer, studying the numbers. "How do you get it?"

"Tell me again," I say.

"Karma's what you make for the future."

"How do you make it?"

I take his bony face and turn him away from the yellow screen in the early morning. All around us is silence.

"It's how you act. I think of it in how you treat somebody, not needing something back. Your mom's an example. I try to wish her well, always wish her well, have a tender place for her, even though she doesn't have many tender places for herself."

He has said this before. And this takes me to a fragment of a memory. "Were you there when I was born?" I say.

Someone told me about that day. A story of a memory of a hospital room. In it is an entire Cambodian family gathered with rice and soda and changes of clothes and blankets, as if they slept there. And baby dresses and diapers.

A baby was born. I think the baby was me.

"I was out fishing," he says. "But you are the cream in my coffee, the one I'd drive all night for."

"Just to buy me shoes." I know how it goes.

I lean back, lift my feet in the air, make him put up his feet to mine. Then we push with all our might and we each claim victory till my knees buckle and we howl.

"Dad," I say, "how can you live without me? Please don't make me live with my mother. How about if I go and see her and take her food?"

He said, "You'll be fine. You are a brilliant, ornery girl."

"You didn't even consider."

I have a whole secret life. And maybe he does. Maybe he has plans all laid out for a place to go when they close the Gulf of Maine.

"This is a family business," I whisper.

"You're the light in my attic," he says. "You're the rabbit in the moon."

The rabbit. I think of the baby in the cottage in the horseshoe of cottages. Luke straddling the chair. Us wishing for a rabbit to give the baby ease. Now my father's leaving. I won't have him to look for rabbits with. What is happening to us?

And all the while I'm remembering the hair falling across Luke Sanna's forehead.

RULES OF THE HOUSE

My father tells me if I go to Rosa's after school, don't stay late. Come on home. I do. My mother and grandmother are sitting on the couch in my father's and my living room. He says, "Tell them the rules of the house. How things run here."

I look from him to my mother to my grandmother. "These are very important," he says to them.

Dad narrows his eyes on my mother in a way that makes it seem that he has two daughters.

My grandmother is tall for a Cambodian woman, the ones I have met. She watches me carefully with her little bird eyes as if I were a new species of person. I vaguely remember—I must have been tiny—playing dress-up in her bright lengths of fabric, the sarongs she wore around the house. And I ate her Cambodian curry. I remember her yellow fingers when she cooked. She does not take her eyes from me.

Today I notice her lips are full and close over her teeth that protrude. She has distinctive high cheekbones. She's wearing lipstick for this occasion. A pale pink lipstick over her full lips.

My mother wears her white coat not zipped. Her face is wide and shimmers with a touch of blush on her cheeks. She's had her hair cut since I saw her, and it comes perfectly at an angle to her chin. It frames dark eyes that dance, looking at my father, who attempts to look at her sternly, but softens. As he does with me. She seems to have the nausea under control and looks like she's on a job interview. Of course, there's the baby.

I'm confused. I turn to my father, questions in my eyes. He can tell he's not getting off that easily.

"You know," he says. "When you're home. Where you go. Tell them all the curfew rules. Don't teenaged girls have curfews? Friends over. Rules for about who can come over."

Dad is in over his head. I feel bad for him. He's trying to leave in the morning. But this is the remaining detail—turn over the daughter.

I say, "Is she moving in, too?"

"Who? Don't be rude."

I glance at my grandmother.

"For the baby," my mother says. "She wants to be here for the baby."

My grandmother still does not take her piercing eyes from me. Her hands rest, one in the other, on her belly.

"Like she took care of you," my mother says.

My eyes flash to my grandmother's hands. Those hands took care of me?

"In Lowell," my mother says.

"You want to make some coffee or something?" Dad says.

"We have two tiny bedrooms," I whisper to him. "How's this going to work?"

He shrugs. Then he says, "I'll pile up the nets I dump in the garage." He and Pete are bringing the nets back that need mending for the next shrimp season. "Give you some room for storing stuff out there if you need." I drop my head in my hands.

"Rules of the house," he says. "Sofie's a good cook. She can cook suppers."

"I'm not a good cook. I only cook one thing." But then I look at this old woman who took care of me. I have the first realization that I have had boundless freedom with Dad, more than I might have with a grandmother who watches me like this old woman is doing. It's time to step in. I sit tall.

"I run the house," I say. "But I'm not here that much. I leave early for school. Dad's leaving me his truck. I work at Dunkin' Donuts till eleven." I'm paving the way to go to the horseshoe of cottages. "And Vincent always wants me to take more hours."

"She's a hard worker," my father assures them. He never quite knew what I did. Or when I did it.

Pilot begins to howl. It's five o'clock, and she always howls at five for her supper. I tell her *hush.* She won't. She's spoiled. She believes, it's getting dark and she's supposed to eat.

"Not every night, but I'm on call."

"For a Dunkin' Donuts?" my mother says. "It's not a hospital." She lifts her chin. "I had a job there one time. We had a schedule."

I begin to seethe.

"I've had every job in the book," my mother says.

"I know," my father says.

This is *not* going well.

"I'll cook," my mother says. "It's easy here. The Asian market's just up there." She can't remember streets. Streets just clutter her mind. She means the main street.

My grandmother says to my father, "She tell her boss nine p.m. on school night." My father looks at me for the answer to this.

"Tell them I often sleep over at Rosa's," I say.

"Well, you can tell them."

I look at my grandmother, who takes me in from what seems like some deep place within her, within the careful way she touches her lips together. Like she has known the world very deeply, including teenaged girls. What was her life like when she was almost seventeen? But I narrow my eyes on her to remind her of her place in this house.

I scoop Pilot's dog kibble into her dish, and she stops howling and I stand with my hands on my hips in the kitchen.

My father stands. “Look, she’s a good girl,” he says. “We’ve been doing just fine. Why don’t you show them the rooms?”

“It’s okay. We can stay in the same room. In Cambodia, didn’t we all sleep in one bed? That’s when my brother and cousins were alive. We slept like a bundle of puppies.” My mother gives us her brimming-with-joy smile that I trust like a snake.

I don’t show them the rooms. What have we done?

Those people in our living room rise, too, and I see that my grandmother, though taller than my mother, has become frail. She rests on my mother, who guides her wobbly steps out the door. I want to stalk her footsteps and warn her right now, *You are not going to stop me from going to see Luke.*

But I wonder. How many brothers and cousins did my mother have? Do we have eyes like they had, when they were alive?

GOOD-BYE

On two index cards, my father left these notes in small black letters, front and back. I find them in the morning when I wake. My father writes in all caps.

Dear Sofie,

I'd drive all night for you. Get along with your mother. She's working to get it together. Once you asked about fear. Your mother has survived more than a human should ever have to imagine. In Cambodia, soldiers took the children away to work in the fields. They starved the people, even the little children. I guess you're old enough to know some of our background. I met your mom when I was working out of Rye Harbor. I nearly got my ear cut off in an accident on the boat. My family had no use for me, but this beautiful girl took care of me. The thing was, she was on the run from a situation in Lowell. I'm not saying it was good or bad, but she moved in and I loved her. But she's got demons that are chasing her. I don't know if she can get free. But I don't give up on a person.

Love,
Dad

On a second card, was he talking more to himself in the wee hours? But he left it.

> My fear is not the day they take our boat. The day I hose her down, paint her hull, haul her nets back to the Heights to mend next winter. Maybe crew for the last fishing boat out of Portsmouth.
>
> My fear is that we shouldn't have called her *Karma*. If you sell your karma, have you sold your soul? But she got me out in the dark all winter, chasing my soul.

I crumple the note in my fist. I did this. I did this.

I'm alone in our house. Nothing looks different. Not the light through the back window. The afghan on the couch, the ball of papers on the desk. My father doesn't take anything. But everything's different. *Who is going to cook for you?* I could have packed meals. At least breakfast to eat after he clears the dogleg. But he loves the expanse of ocean and horizon. For him, all the problems on shore fall away.

The government, the daughter, the daughter's mother with demons. I imagine speeding through the snow roads down to the co-op, boarding the *Karma* just in time. Tell him, Dad, we're going to be okay! Steam back in tonight. I'll make chowder and biscuits. At least wait till spring. Wait. But he'd get back here. Be grounded all February since the season is closed. Grow a jagged beard. Follow the marine report. Watch the bend of the birch trees. Fishing. There's no going forward. There's no going back. We go round and round. Sinking.

I can't see my father opening a Dunkin' Donuts at 4:00 a.m. Doing the crossword in between Mrs. Bennett's cream filled and the kids' double sugars like Vincent. Growing bitter. That's what grounded looks like.

Pilot and I plow a path into the new snow, heading down to the river. Once more I stand on the skeleton beams of the pier. The wind cuts into my face and my neck. Pilot races through the strip of horizon.

Alone in our house, I shower. It's taking my mother and grandmother some time to get organized, so I have one day alone. I imagine my family crowding beside me, around me. Puppies in a bed. I dress. I sit on my bed and brush my hair. I lay my hands on my belly. It feels jumpy with tension, the way my father described the sea. I hear every sound in the house without him.

I look at my hands and suddenly see my grandmother's hands—Yiey, as my father calls her. She sat with one palm lightly over the other as they rested on her belly. Like mine.

Rosa gives me a ride to the co-op to pick up my father's truck before school. I go to Mr. Murray's class, but I don't want any of the world he'll offer to me. My world is closed in. Now it's February. A long dark month. As my father steams south, he'll have only the new moon above.

MY MOTHER'S PARTY

My mother invited me to a party with Cambodians the night before they move in.

I go only for the purpose of establishing control with my mother and grandmother. I'll tell them what time to come. Tell them where they can and cannot park. They have been staying with another Cambodian family in the next town, and the house where I go smells like garlic and ginger and fish paste.

In the kitchen, my grandmother spreads open wrappers for egg rolls. The men are drinking beer in one room. The women work and talk in another.

"I tell the police, take him. He is my son, but I cannot control him. You take him."

"The police will send him back to Cambodia."

"He will die." The women fall into the Khmer language.

Then the mother returns to English. "Only half die," she says. "The other half, they grow crazy. I turn my back on him. I say to my son, why are your eyes red? Why do you steal the dollars I earn helping old people bathe their bodies?"

"You be careful," my grandmother says to me.

"What?" I say, startled. Her eyes frighten me. They are an emergency. Everything she looks at could be on fire.

"Be careful." She raises the volume. "Stay away from boy

who do drug like they say. Boy who drink too much." She speaks sharply at me while the women talk in the language I don't understand. I back away. I'm wearing khakis and a tank top because I told Vincent I could fill in after this and am half dressed for work. I can fly out the door.

The host of honor hasn't come. *Now,* I think. *I'll go now.* "I'll be home from school by four tomorrow. You can come then," I say to my grandmother.

She hands me a mango with something in the glint of her eye that says, *This* is what's important.

"You are Cambodian, too," she says. She gives me a knife.

"Where's my mother?" I say. "Isn't this her party?"

"It is not today. It will be another day."

No one knows what day. No one knows where my mother is. Why are Cambodians so crazy? How long have these women been in this country and they still don't speak English?

"You are hungry," my grandmother says. The women are looking at her and me. "You eat before go to work." Her eyes turn agitated.

A woman looks at me and demands to know, "You are Leap granddaughter?"

Leap is my grandmother's name. "Leap's," I say. "I am Leap's granddaughter."

"Do you know what they do to Leap mother?"

"Sophea, I tell you later," my grandmother says.

"What did they do?" I say. I know they mean the soldiers, the Khmer Rouge. Maybe old people have told this story before. I don't remember. Maybe I wasn't there. Maybe I didn't listen. Today I listen. Luke makes me want to understand what happens to people far away in war. With Luke, I am a Cambodian girl. Someone brings me a Cambodian beer. I take a very long drink.

My grandmother continues to slice vegetables for the egg rolls. I slice the fruit from the mangoes, very clumsily.

"Like this," she says. She guides the sharp blade with her thumb, lifting the skin along the curve of the mango. I continue, following her example.

The storyteller begins. "Her mother, in Cambodia, the Khmer Rouge say she too old, she do not work. Do not feed her. If you feed her, we will not feed you, too. They starve her to death."

My grandmother's and my fingers hold the knives with skill as we cut.

"Every day she brush Leap hair until she cannot lift her hand. She still miss her."

This makes no sense to me. "Why didn't you take her food when they weren't looking?" I ask my grandmother.

"The guard is a boy with an ax. He starving, too. They promise him rice if he will guard. His life or Leap mother. He can choose."

My grandmother stirs pork that sizzles in a black skillet.

"Every day she do Leap hair. The boy watch."

I drink the Cambodian beer. "You are telling folktales," I say, heavy-headed instantly from the beer.

"Is not a *tale*. This *happen*." The woman is angry. She shouts, "She beg for food. She say, 'If I could just taste food one more time.'

"Your grandmother bring her rice she hide in her scarf and the boy is sleep. Mother eyes shine with happiness to taste the rice. She eat it all, even if her body look like sticks and she does not stay alive. For this, she love your grandmother."

She said this very loud, a few inches from my face. I shut my eyes. I see the image of sticks on the ground, one stick holding a brush. And I have stepped out of this world. I make myself open my eyes and be here in this kitchen in New Hampshire even though I am spinning with the beer.

I turn to my grandmother, who swiftly grates gingerroot across the tines of a fork. But her face is unchanged. It is as if she did not listen. Or that story is in her bones and tissues and the air she breathes and she lives in that other world all the time. I don't know what to do with this. My grandmother touches my hair. I feel the pressure of her hand on my head and I spin. I fill the egg roll wrappers with the sliced cabbage, ginger, and a little of my blood because I am not fast enough for my grandmother and I have rushed the knife. I toss in the pork in small pieces.

My grandmother folds them and drops the egg rolls into boiling oil. In the fryer, the oil bubbles around them. The smell makes a burning in my throat. "When I come," she says, "I tell you more folktale."

THAT SONG

Rosa has come because she couldn't find me at school. I'm on the couch in my living room, the weight of my dog on my feet.

"I feel sick, Rosa. I am sick." But then I can't remember what I'm saying.

Rosa puts her arm around my shoulder. "Come to school," she says.

"How can I go to school?"

"You have to pull yourself together."

Luke sent me a text. *Can you come tonight?*

"I'll make you some breakfast. And then maybe you'll hear what you're saying."

"Cambodian beer," I whisper.

"Is it good?"

I shake my head and my mind spins and spins and spins.

But I can see the words on my phone. *Can you come? I would like to see your eyes.*

"Do I still live here? Where's my father?"

"You must have been really drunk," Rosa says.

"Must have," I say.

"How did you get here? You said you were going to some party. At your mother's."

I'm forced to try and remember. "My mother," I say. "I

came with her. She's here somewhere. Maybe she's in my father's bedroom."

"It must have started off bad," Rosa says. "Rooming with your mother."

"She is just . . ." I pause. ". . . crazy." I am beginning to come back to the house, to the light streaming into the back window, to my mother. And my grandmother.

Or I could meet you on the strip. By the statue. I'll read Kerouac to you.

The morning sun lifts.

"Sing me that song, Rosa, about the Spanish dancer."

But then a river of light blinds me. It is beautiful and dazzling.

Rosa hums while she tries to get us going. I remember pictures of beautiful Cambodia on the wall last night with my grandmother. Is beauty still beauty when you are starving? No, not if the morning sun brings the boy hauling his ax to guard an old woman to make sure she is starving, since then he'll get food to keep himself alive.

"Do you think your mom and your dad are getting back together?" Rosa says.

Again, I try to come back to the river where I live. I focus on Rosa in the kitchen. She wears a gauzy white shirt and turquoise hoops in her ears. "You're such a romantic, Rosa."

"I can't help it."

"Do you have any condoms?" I say.

She is popping toast from the toaster, spreading it with butter. She knows this is a life-defining question. But we both know things we have not talked about. She nods.

"Did I call in last night? God, I hope so. I think I did, before I knew I couldn't drive."

Instead of my grandmother's fierce bird eyes, I see her composed lips, how they gently meet. I think of how even her lips, her whole body, must hold the memory of the story her friend told.

I pick up my phone. *After work. Your cottage.*

CHECK THE WIND

I *had* called in last night. Oh, Jesus, I'm relieved. I still have a job. At five p.m., wind cracks a branch from a tree and hurls it onto Woodbury Avenue. The temperature is so low, the truck groans. Streetlights show ribbons of ice in the trees. In my father's coat, I pick my way over ice from the truck to the door of the shop. I hold the door from the wind and find haven in Dunkin' Donuts with my hair pressed to my face.

"You're late," Vincent says.

I'm relieved to see his jowly jaw. "Sorry," I say, shedding the slicker and shaking out my arms. I wipe my face with my cocked elbow. Thank god nobody is here, just Mrs. Bennett, who holds a small coffee cup with grace. The streetlight features one side of her face and silver hair, the other side in shadow.

"I'll make it up," I say breathlessly. I smell the cold wool of my sweater as I pull it over my head. I say, "I'll stay and close on Saturday if you want."

Vincent doesn't answer. He goes back to the crossword folded on his clipboard. I hear the sound of the black fine-point marker scratching across the squares.

"Thursday," I say. Puzzles get worth doing on Thursdays.

"Yup," he says.

Maybe I'm not here. Maybe I don't exist. Maybe I am that

ghost in the tree the Cambodians talk about. Except I can't be that with Luke. With Luke, I am all body. I am nothing but my body. Fingertips. Shoulders, throat. My mind softens.

Vincent zips along, filling in tiny black letters. I pull my hair into a ponytail and put on the cap. Wet strings of hair slip down. What story am I made of? I check the coffee pots and brew a new pot of dark roast. It is already black outside the window. Desperate people come in for coffee in the middle of storm winds.

I text, *Dad, how's the wind*?

I check the other pots. The counter shines with jimmies and circles of milk under the fluorescent lights, and I wipe it down. My phone signals. *Steady. You are in the storm. Stay where you are.*

Yes.

I know I'm going to Luke's tonight. My mother has been at my house all day. I don't know what her routine will be in the night, if she'll stretch out under the afghan and sleep after dinner. I don't know what she cooked for dinner. I don't know what my father's room looks like now that it's hers.

"Vincent," I say.

"Mm," he says. He's growing a sprout of a beard on his chin.

"Do you believe things happen for a reason? You know, the belief that there's a universe and we're just here tonight in a storm, with all of our problems, but there's some reason why we're here. Some . . . I don't know." I make circles with my hands. "Some shape?"

"You mean like fatalism. Over my head, babe."

"Don't call me babe. Is that what fatalism is? Like things aren't random?"

A siren sounds from the snow-packed street.

"You're talking to a guy who grew up on Alice in Chains. But you know what I think? I think we use about a fraction of our brains, and there's a whole lot going on we don't know about, like a reality outside our frequency." Vincent writes "100 percent" in tiny letters at the top of his crossword. Then "A+."

I almost ask him, "Vincent, do you write those messages about your lost love on the seawall?"

At Rye Cottages, I check the wind in a stand of birch trees like I always do when my father heads into the sea, the unknown. Winds are building. Branches are swaying. I worry because now the electric wire begins to whistle. Could be gusting to thirty knots off shore. But I'm here.

LEAVE YOUR SLEEP

I changed to my jeans and sweater after work, same black lace-up boots. I put on eyeliner, green, all around, which is how I picture the Spanish dancer. I am someone different tonight. Will life continue its normal progression at school at seven thirty in the morning? And will I continue?

Luke is bundled into a padded olive-drab jacket.

"Let's walk," he says, not looking at me.

"The wind bends you sideways," I say.

He touches my hand. My hand.

"I'll show you the boat I'm planning to go fishing on."

"I don't go on boats," I say. "I don't go on water."

"Why?"

"I've always been afraid of water."

He doesn't question this. He doesn't say my fear is unreasonable, just a phobia—here are ten steps to conquer your fear. I like how I say something, and he listens—he accepts it. What would he do if I told him the story about starving a woman? If I could find the words to repeat it. My great-grandmother. But he is the only one I could imagine telling this terror to. Maybe because what he did is raw in his eyes.

I glance at Luke as we walk. He doesn't wear a hat, and the wind whips his hair.

"There's something I have to tell you," he says.

I am uneasy to hear. But I lean my head in to him in the wind that rushes us forward.

"I've been out a few months, back from Afghanistan longer, but every night, I'm there," he says. "Every night I'm on the same patrol. Every night." He shouts the words in the wind, and somehow it makes them more impersonal. More okay to say. He puts his bare hand on the metal of a guardrail that I know could take off a layer of skin, but he pulls his hand away and does not even grimace. "My head keeps me playing out scenes, trying to change the end," he says. "With your father I was too busy to think." The words are stark in the cold air as we march. "This kid dies. I dream it over and over and over."

We have reached the road before the harbor. I turn down in. He follows. We come to a house with a glassed-in porch facing the breakwater. The fishing boats rock at their moorings across from the breakwater. We hear the steady horn of a buoy. The cold seems to free him to talk. A cocoon of cold.

"You got to be fast when you get them out. No time to stop. No time to ask. No time to say, 'Fuck, I don't know what to do.' You can never hesitate. This guy's heart will quit. You're gonna lose him.

"Sometimes I dream I go in ten times, a hundred times. Every time I think this time I'll save him . . . give me one more time. The kid is screaming."

"You mean a child?"

"No, young kid, eighteen, a soldier."

I imagine the fear of closing my eyes to try to sleep when it means you are going to live that again, that second of the possibility that you could save him. Someone is screaming. I stand very close so I can listen. At the same time I remember. I remember, very young, waking in my mother's house and someone is screaming. It woke me and I raced to her bed. I needed to keep her, don't leave me alone. Did we sit in the dark in a huddle, my mother who was screaming and me, and I pointed my finger for her to look at the moon?

Beyond the jetty, Luke and I see the fishing boats jostling and banging in the wind. One would be the boat Luke's going out on.

I say, "I'd go on a boat if I could. I'd fish with my father." I want to talk about the boat.

"Every second," he says, "you got to know what to do. I don't have any respect for a person who . . . there's no time to say, 'Fuck, what's next?' Your father's like that, he always knows, you and your father." He is slowing down. The words start slowing down. How does he know me?

The wind shoves us. And under the black sky I grab his hand and we race on the edge of the icy road, piercing the snow with our boots. We race back to Luke's cottage.

We stand in the dark inside his door.

"Did I scare you?" he says.

"No."

Around us is silence.

The cottage's heat makes me ache as I begin to thaw. I see my grandmother's eyes. I feel her brushing my hair.

Luke takes my hands, warms them in his bare hands that are somehow warm. "Some things you shouldn't know."

He takes off my coat, unlaces my boots. I feel his fingers carefully unknot each lace while I lean against the door, my palms pressed into the cold wood.

His touches my face. I don't decide what to do in my head so much as in my body.

I step in to him, and his breath is warm on my cheek.

We stand in the pale light scattered by frost on the window. I feel his hips on mine. I let my hands wrap around him and hold him. He is so still that I think we will explode. I am pressing back, pressing into him. He holds me slightly away. We breathe.

Then he fits his body together with mine. He finds my lips

and kisses me. Slow and deep and rocking and aching. And I am transformed, like the seal who becomes a woman.

I return his kiss in the way he teaches me, and it is as if we are discovering the universe.

"Jesus," I whisper. And he laughs and we fall down onto a couch that squeals and kills us with its springs. But I am too far gone with kissing. The discovery of kissing. And his body. And mine.

In exhaustion, he had fallen asleep on the bumpy couch. He whispers directions in my ear. "Hold on. You just got the good stuff. You're the braveheart guy. As soon as they drop the line, you're going up. Buddy!" Now he shouts the name Buddy.

I stand. "Luke, you're dreaming!" I say. "Luke!"

Luke jumps from the couch. He lets out a moan like an animal. And then, "Aw, god." He's catching his breath. His black hair falls over his eyes.

I see something on his bedside table. My tiger's eye shines. My ring. It had been in his shirt pocket. But what time is it? I have to get out of here.

"I never know where I am. Just keep talking to me. Are you okay?" He is alarmed. "Christ, I didn't hurt you?"

"You kissed me," I say. "I kissed you. I never even did that with someone before." I wish I hadn't said it. I sound like a child.

"I thought— Jesus, I'm sorry," he says. "I startle bad. Sometimes if I sleep I wake up and we're under attack."

"You were just talking," I say. "I was Buddy. You called me Buddy." I feel the ring of the condom in my hip pocket. Who am I? "I'll bring rice." I'm putting on my coat. "Rice is good for nightmares." How do I know this? "With ginger. Ginger is for pain. I'll bring gingerroot to get through the night."

I am telling remedies that somehow I know.

He is sitting on the edge of the bed, his head bent into his hands. His shoulders are so tight, I think if I touch him, he would snap like a wire bearing the weight of one of the tankers from Romania that come into the harbor.

"Turmeric is also for pain," I tell him. "Garlic for earaches." I pull on my boots.

"Are you okay?" he asks.

I try to think of what I am. I say, "I never wanted to be with anybody before."

He sighs. I sit tight beside him.

"I'm seeing a mess of ginger trees in here," he says. His voice is husky.

I rest my chin in the curve of his neck. We fit together.

THEY WILL SEND YOU BACK

I had not called my mother. I am used to my father leaving at all hours to go fishing. It never mattered when I came home, though I always came. Until Luke.

I slip in the door past the stack of gear by the house. It's midnight. I almost trip over Pilot, who is right by the door, as if she is on guard. As if she needed to warn me. She whines, and I hear her tail beat on the floor. I kneel to stroke her. She paces from me to my father's bedroom door. The house seems like someone else's house. It smells like someone else's house. Their stuff smells different from my father's and mine.

I stay on the floor with my dog, not wanting to go farther. I belong more with Luke than here in what should be my own house. I am so tired, though, and want to climb the stairs to my bed.

I think my mother is asleep in the bedroom, but she calls out. "Would you help me turn over?" she says. "Where have you been?" I force myself to enter the room. I lean beside the bed, and she wraps her fingers around my arms above the elbows. She pulls until she is on her side. "I can't sleep on my back or my belly. He's been kicking all night."

"Shhh, Mom, now you're on your side. Go to sleep."

Her long black hair falls over her face. "Where have you been?" she says.

I tell her, "Get a little more sleep."

My mother calls from the bedroom, maybe from out of a dream, "If you are in trouble with the law, they will send you back." I remember the women talking at the Cambodian's house. A mother had given up on her drug-using son.

They will send you back. The phrase replays. They will send you back.

In the morning I wake from a dream I don't remember. But I wake up left alone, my heart panicked. I wake missing people. I miss myself, the girl I was. I miss my house with my father. I sit in the kitchen with Pilot. I sit cross-legged on the floor like a child, watching her gobble her kibble.

"Good girl," I say. "I have to leave you again to go to school."

Pilot wags her tail to hear me talk to her. The story comes back to me while she gobbles. How could you forbid someone to eat? When you're hungry, that's all your mind can hold. Hunger. Hunger. That's all there is. I must have food. What do you do with that fear, not of starving, but that a soldier could control you so completely to be able to say, *For this one! Nothing.* And there is no one not afraid.

MY SON, RITHY

"I old," Yiey says. She has been lugging plastic bags from my mother's car.

"Not that old," I say. It's Saturday morning, and I need to get to work. But she is tired and asks for a cup of tea. I put the kettle on. She settles into a small chair by the window, overlooking bare trees.

"When I see you, I remember my mother. She tall like you." I pause, my hand rattles the cups. Can't she see I'm half out the door? But my grandmother is old and wants to remember. She says, "Everyday, my mother tie my hair."

I say I know, she already told me.

"It is so hot in Cambodia. She tie my hair in a scarf before I go to work in the field."

"How old were you?" I ask.

"Maybe nineteen. I have two baby."

One was my mother.

The kettle screams.

"Who was your other baby?"

She said, "Rithy, my son."

"Where's he?"

I bring her the cup of tea. I tie up my boots.

"In Pol Pot time," she says. "We have no food. You work in

the field or they kill you. Khmer Rouge soldier promise us rice for our kid. But no rice. All the food, they give the Khmer Rouge. They don't care if we die. They give us water with grains of rice. This is not enough food.

"Rithy sneak from the hut—past the Khmer Rouge guard—to go hunting. Everybody think we will not see him again. But in hour he sneak past the guard again, his scarf full of cricket. A hundred cricket! Your mother pounce on the cricket, stuffing cricket in her mouth."

My grandmother shows me with her hands and her teeth, how fast they stuffed the crickets in their mouths. In my mouth I imagine the crunch of the crickets' legs. I try to imagine my mother. How old was she? Stuffing her mouth with crickets.

"He save their live. My son. He know where to hunt cricket."

The story spins around me, but I have no room for crickets in my memories. It is one of the little secrets my mother never talked about. I don't know where to put them. It is a story wrapped in the smells of turmeric and peppers. They saved my mother's life. This story I'll tell Luke. He'll understand the crickets even if his memories are already full of dying. And he might whisper to me, "Some things you shouldn't know."

HEADLIGHTS

For a few days, I try out plans in my head to go to see Luke again, with potions for nightmares and sleep and a bounding dog. Rosa and I hang out downtown on Sunday. We study in the library. I don't want to go home. I want to stay in my world. We call my father and gossip with him about school. He says he'll try to borrow his deckhand's car and drive home on my birthday. Rosa teases him that the teachers all miss him. "They're pining," she says. "They've got it bad for you, Johnny."

We hold the phone up between us, and I hear him laugh and that makes me sink down in my chair and grin like a kid. I say, "I'd drive all night."

And he says, "You're not calling from a Laundromat?"

"No, Dad."

"What's that about a Laundromat?" Rosa says after we scream "I LOVE YOU" into the phone and hang up.

"One time my mother forgot me at a Laundromat in Lowell. Someone had to call my father to come pick me up. She just forgot I was with her. She pulled away from the Laundromat. I remember her headlights pulling away and I raced after the headlights but I couldn't catch her. I went back to the Laundromat. It was dark, and I thought the world had ended."

"How old were you?"

"Four."

"She forgot you? You were four?"

"Well, Dad drove from Portsmouth. Somebody called him. He took me to her and they had a long talk. That's when I heard the letters *PTSD*."

We are scuffing through snow. We've got to get to the homework, which has been sliding.

But I'm not thinking of homework. This story is one more thing I seem to be stockpiling. I have a stash—my tiger's eye ring Luke keeps in his right chest pocket. One of Pilot's puppy teeth. A whelk shell I found on the beach beneath the 95 bridge. My mother's voice when she sang to me in Khmer, which I don't want, but it's coming.

"I didn't know what PTSD spelled," I tell Rosa. "It just meant your mother could vanish and you'd be alone."

We scuff along. Rosa is quiet, and I hope I didn't upset her. But all she says is, "I think I love Johnny. I want to marry him, after I'm a star." And we howl.

"I had a stuffed rabbit," I say. "I remember that rabbit. I was wheeling it around in one of those canvas baskets in the Laundromat and singing at the top of my voice to make her remember me."

HEAT

The next day I go to Luke's after school with supplies. I have a large bag of basmati rice, which I've always craved, and jasmine tea, and a chunk of gingerroot. I will go home by nine o'clock, but my mother and I won't have anything to talk about. When I go home, I'll go to my room with Pilot and text Rosa and my father, in the dark, so my mother doesn't know I'm awake.

Luke's cheek is bruised red and purple, and his left eye that was beginning to lose its purple ring is now puffed up. His shirt is shredded in the back, and a splint and thick bandage hold his left ring finger immobilized. He doesn't want to talk about it, his Saturday night.

"How I lost my last job," is all he'll say about it. He grins. "Partying."

I wince at the tender skin as he peers at me.

"We're celebrating," he says, showing me a counter full of grocery bags. "The new boat I'm going on. And I'm cooking you dinner."

He is changed. Solemn, despite the bravado. But he is meticulous with his hands as he lifts the vegetables from the bags and lines them up on the counter. The counter becomes a still life. Luke talks about the captain he'll fish with out of Rye going for scallops. I tell him about my father, who's already fishing on

Chincoteague. "Monkfish, he says. He says the landings haven't been bad."

Luke pulls out a chair. He wants me to sit. I can tell he is aware of every move I make even when he's not looking at me. "Don't you have some homework?" he says.

"Yeah," I say. I drop my pack on the table.

"You got half an hour."

I unload the pack. I begin to write an assignment on my iPad, but I'm aware that Luke is quickly and surely slicing mushrooms, red onion, an orange pepper, in spite of his splint.

"What are you writing about?" he asks. His hands do the ordinary job of cutting slim wedges of carrots. They draw my focus, and I think less about where he was last night, who beat him up, what he might have done to the other guy.

"A premier moon."

"What's a premier moon?"

"Waxing."

"Not waning?"

"You can tell. If it's a premier moon, there's a line on the left like the letter P. It's for astronomy. My father was always pointing out things in the sky, what fishermen see when there's only the sea and the sky."

"It's been just you and him?" Luke says.

"I don't need a mother," I say. "Where's yours?"

Silence. Then, "By her phone. I'm killing her."

This is the second time he's mentioned his family. The first time, it was about the journey home place—Project Odyssey. Some place his family wants him to go. Do I have anything to do with why he's here, and not going there for help? A flash of a thought. I want the thought to disappear as fast as it came. But it stays in the back of my mind.

"You didn't know I was a chef," he says. "Impressed as hell?"

Luke drops the perfectly angled carrots into a skillet with wedges of mushroom.

He comes and kisses me square on the lips. He smells like sex. What I think sex must be. I open my mouth to him. For as long as he'll let me. I am sitting in a white wooden chair at the table, books spread across. He is on his knees, I turn and bend to him, his arms around my hair. Slow. We breathe each other in. For this second, I stop running after something. All that exists is the sweet heat in my body touching the sweet heat of him.

He pulls away. Is this—I almost cry—what desire is? It is hard for us to bear.

"What else do you write about?" he says, stepping back, so far back I must feel like a bomb to him. He adjusts his shoulders, his back.

I stand. I go to the window where dark has descended. "You're trying to make me the child. You're trying to put me there. It's too late."

He doesn't answer. I return to my screen. My mind is fuzzy. I feel drunk and I didn't drink anything. Should I just go?

The sauce Luke made is simmering, and he takes out some pencils and pieces of cardboard leaning against the shelves. I had seen these the first time I came. I hear scratches across the cardboard as he sketches. I look up. He leans over the cardboard, his elbow around it, tender, almost like it's a cradle. And he draws.

I don't leave. "Oceans," I say, burying my face in my work. "I also write about oceans. You show me a fish, dead or alive, I can identify the species. I could be an inspector for the government, but my father says I'd be a traitor."

Luke opens the oven door, and a blast of heat escapes as well as the aroma of roasting chicken. With a wide metal spoon he bastes the chicken's skin. It is golden. Luke is wearing jeans and just a T-shirt in the heat of the woodstove and the oven.

Outside, we are bounded by snow. The night is bitter cold but clear. The smell of the golden chicken fills the cabin.

"Can you stay?" he says. I know he means later, longer than I have before. The words are almost buried in the heat of the oven and slam of the door. We both know I can't, but I see he doesn't know what to do about me. I think he has gotten used to me. What he didn't want to do. The way I'm used to him.

Luke straddles a chair again. He likes to have a chair between us. He rubs his palms across his head and studies me. It seems like a moment I could bring up one thing besides sex that is on my mind. Does he still have the gun?

But he says, "There's a guy on a boat out of Rye. He sells straight from the boat." I had told him about my illegal sales.

"That's Ned," I say. "He's got a CSF. He has all the permits to sell, and people buy shares of his catch. He's got a scallop license, takes him through winter."

We eat the feast Luke has prepared. And then I stumble into research, cross-legged on the couch. Community supported fisheries. These are legal ways fishermen can sell their fish. I find site after site. What do we need from the feds? What do we need from the state? What's a sole proprietorship? This night gives me the spark of a dream for May, when my father comes home.

I look up at Luke, who is sketching as I tap. He is beautiful in his concentration, again with his arm almost tenderly around his work. I stand to look. He is sketching this cabin. This room with details precisely shown in miniature. Half of the orange pepper he left unsliced, three pepper seeds beside it, the nubby bumpy texture of the rows on the cotton bedspread, the tiger's eye in my ring, the cross-stitched map on the wall of the state of New Hampshire with tiny crosses to make its shape, a girl in profile, her hair falling over her shoulder. I think he has drawn my mother but then realize that he has drawn me. He sees that I see it. He keeps sketching in details.

I am suddenly grateful that my father isn't here, and he can't see my face when I look at Luke or see me when I come home and my mind is on Luke's cradling arm.

It's late, I notice, and it's always time. I slowly begin to pack up.

"Can you stand hanging out with me?" Luke asks me.

I look at his green eyes and remember when I first saw them, when he took off his sunglasses on the beach. It was the most intimate moment of my life, when he showed me his eyes.

I start putting on my layers. "It's so funny with you," I say. I wrap my scarf around my neck and lips, preparing for the cold.

"Don't do that," he says. He lifts my hair from under the scarf, and the scarf falls to my shoulders, below my chin. His eyes are narrowed. I kiss him.

"We were all covered there." He's trying to explain. "I wore a neck gaiter for the dust, armor, covered head to toe, like the women."

"Everything about you is familiar," I say. I stand, hands on my hips, studying him, my coat unzipped, one boot on. Undone. "Even things I don't know anything about are familiar. Like gaiters. What's a gaiter?"

He makes circles with his thumb and pointer finger upside down around his eyes, his pinkies stretched from his jaw, his elbows wide, and he is goofy like a clown and I laugh out loud. "Gaiters and goggles," he says. We are both laughing.

I wrap my arms around his neck, and we fall silent. Suddenly I say, "Is this what love is?" I want him to look at it, this ache and hunger and being on the edge of tears, like I could hold it in my hand and we could wonder at it. What is this?

He wraps his arm around my hair and holds me hard to him, and I feel his deep letting go of breath. "I don't know," he says. "Tell me you're okay."

I don't know how to answer. It's not about being okay. Mr. Murray uses the phrase "essential detail." Every word we speak, every gesture we make, the smell of his body and mine with his, even those little seeds of the pepper, they're the essential details that are my life.

"I'm with you," I say.

SAVING PILOT'S LIFE

I am on the couch reading, my arm around my dog, her nose resting on my knee.

"That dog," my mother says.

"What about that dog?" I say.

"I can hardly sleep with him around barking." My mother says, "You leave that dog with me too much. Yiey will decide to cook him."

I know she likes to scare me, but this is worse than saying the police will send me back to Cambodia where I have never lived. And besides I am Scottish, which I will tell the police.

"I chain her up outside. A dog should be outside."

I throw the book down. "You chain her? Pilot?"

"In the house she howls. She stands at the window and howls, looking for you. So I chain her outside. She howls there. But I put on the music."

"You can't chain her. She's used to people. She can't be alone outside." I am spitting like a cat ready to fight. "Don't you ever!" I shout. "This is our house."

I call my father. "Lydia says that my grandmother will cook her."

"Who, Sofie?"

"Pilot!" I tell him.

"She's not going to cook the dog," my father says, like he has heard this before. "Your mother gets angry and she says things she doesn't mean. Maybe some of these things you need to work out at your end."

"I can't believe you left me with these people!"

"They are not 'these people.' They are family."

"You're in Chincoteague. What do you know? What do you know about these people? You left us."

I am so upset as I hang up. I can't let go of being angry. "She's a girl," I say to my mother. "Pilot's a girl! You said 'him.' You called her *him*."

"He's dinner if you don't watch out."

"She's a girl!"

My mother is trying to get to the bathroom, holding on to the furniture because she cannot see her feet or what is in front of them.

I want her out of here. But all her stuff in the world is in my father's bedroom. I think of the few things I have stockpiled and how I could walk out that door in a heartbeat. But I'm not letting her kick me out of my house.

"Mom." I try to shove my anger back down my throat. I have to say this calmly. I practice not hissing through her long stream of pee. She returns. Throughout all of this, Pilot is turning her eyes from one of us to the other. It is almost time for her dinner, and soon she will howl to remind us.

"Mom, do you want me to drive you to the doctor all the days next week you have to go?"

"Yes," she says. Not a breath of hesitation. Her eyes light. It won't last.

"Tell me the days."

"They tell me. I don't know."

"Okay, when you get an appointment I won't go to school. I will stay with you and we'll go to the doctor."

"And you will sit with me?"

When I was three I put my hand on her arm. *Stay with me.*

"Yes. You just have to call in my excuse," I say.

"What is your excuse?" my mother says.

Words run through my mind. Insanity, Pol Pot, Chincoteague, saving the pure heart of my dog that I love. "Say family emergency."

"We are an emergency," my mother says. "All the time."

"And you will keep anything from happening to Pilot on the other days, the days I am in school. And you won't chain her outside."

"What about all the days you are with the soldier?"

I had started emptying the dishwasher so I didn't have to watch how hard it was for her to move around, to bend over, being so suddenly huge. But my hand stops with a glass on the edge of a shelf. I want to say, *What soldier?* But she is too sure.

"Do you think I'm deaf, when you and Rosa talk?"

I ease around her and her belly and her almond eyes lined with black.

"You have no right," I say.

She winces. "I have heartburn," she says. "Everything I eat causes heartburn."

Then I decide. This is my house. I can do what I want. She is not my mother, and I have no reason to hide. "His name is Lucas Sanna," I say.

"So those days too," she says.

"Yes, you have to protect Pilot those days, too."

She frowns.

"I am sixteen." I don't need to justify.

"Don't be like me," she says.

The thought horrifies me. "You were with my father when you were sixteen. That was your best time." That was cruel. But I don't stop. "What is it about the Bong guy you keep going back to in Lowell? What's he got over you? Grow up!"

She rubs her belly. Swaybacked, she lowers her body, gingerly, slowly, to the couch. When she's not yelling at me, as in this single second, I see how sad her eyes are. But I have too much anger toward her to care. It's her own fault. She's had lots of chances. And now she acts like my father gave her my house.

I BRUSH YOU

My grandmother sleeps in my father's room with my mother. In my imagination, she comes to me in Luke's cabin. I keep pushing her away, but she comes back. And I can't push away the secrets she has told me.

They must be secrets. No one told me about crickets in the war. In school, we studied genocide. We studied war propaganda and the hope for what communism could bring in tiny Cambodia. For my family, I think their war comes at night. And in the day, they stuff it all in a pot and try again to live with each other. I'm what comes from it all. A rabbit running from them.

Yiey and my mother have brought taro chips and sweet and sour lotus rootlets into the kitchen, and ginger tea and cardamom, and the house has taken on these smells, too.

I am sitting with Pilot curled next to me in sleep. It's dark, and Yiey and I can see each other by a streak of moonlight. Yiey sits on the couch, brushing her long hair. There is something about her stern face that makes me be still. I look at her lips that try to close over her teeth, and I think of her mother in Cambodia. What if she talks about Cambodia? What if she talks about the crickets?

But she doesn't talk. She offers to brush my hair. "I brush you." I shake my head no. But I don't leave. I think about my great-grandmother, my father's grandmother, who gave me her 1920s silver hairbrush she got from her mother. I add it to the picture, the way Luke added the angle of the ratty paperbacks to his sketch. My hairbrush has a round silver body with spots of tarnish and a slender handle. It is side by side with my whelk shell. Some of the horsehair bristles are broken off.

I look at Yiey. She's not doing it, but I can almost feel her brush pull through my hair. Yiey's mother brushed her hair, the women said at the party, until she was too weak and begged to taste rice once more.

This story terrifies me so much I can understand wanting the gun that is somewhere in Luke's cabin to be able to wipe out the memory of that mother brushing my hair. How can my grandmother have this terrible memory and yet still have the peace of the sea in her bearing?

PAINTINGS

Luke's duffel has been packed from the first time I came here, as if every day he decides if he should go or stay. In his duffel are a camouflage cap with earflaps, army clothes, chaps, spikes for his boots. The gun is not there. Also in the duffel is a tin that holds pencils for drawing. The disassembled sides, bottoms, and flaps of boxes he draws on are behind the bag. There are sketches and bright paintings he does with watercolors that he uses still thick from the tube. His drawings are of footprints, tracks, long shadows in the snow, my hair falling over my shoulder, our cabin, a courtyard in Afghanistan with some people he must have known.

On the night I study the paintings, I tell Luke my grandmother's story about the crickets. And later, when he's gone for only a second to pick up some food, I find the gun. For the past four weeks I've imagined it. My hand is on the Kerouac books on the shelf of raggedy paperbacks. *On the Road* and *Maggie Cassidy*. I wanted to read the one about Maggie. On the cover a girl leans over a guy in a field with the Lowell skyline behind them. *A novel of first love*, it says beneath the title.

I see the gun when I pick up *Maggie Cassidy*. It's the length of my hand. I know because as I replace the book on the shelf, I let my hand slide over to the gun and feel the shape of its handle. It's silver and brown, and longer than the paperback. The gun sits behind the books, looking out.

Something else is by the bookshelf. Three more pieces of cardboard, cut in Luke's careful way, identical in size. They lean against the shelf. I see a painting of a soldier holding a child. I can't see the child's face or the soldier's. I see the child's fist. A girl, I wonder, since Luke put the tiniest smudge of red on the nails. But you can tell it's a child because the fist is small and pudgy. I understand the soldier's focus by the way he leans his head to her, even though he's covered in gear. His hands are in thin black gloves. Two fingers touch the child's wrist at her pulse. He's a medic.

I can't take my eyes away. An American flag in black and white is on his helmet.

The second painting is so meticulous in its detail, it could have been a photo. It's of a very large bandage wrapped around a torso—there is only the torso. Two hands twist the bandage into a white bar. I can see the stretchy ridges of fabric and where it turns to blood.

The last is the angel child from Luke's phone. His mother had sent her picture, his sister who had written, *Do you remember me?*

I return to the pot of rice I was cooking on the stove.

Later, we eat the rice and shrimp and Luke's stir-fry, and I am so hungry I devour the food. All the while I see the image of the child's fist and the black gloves on her pulse. Luke asks me to repeat the story that happened in a hut on stilts in Cambodia before either of us was born. He doesn't take his eyes from me.

He had not hidden his paintings. They lean against the shelf with *Maggie Cassidy,* with the gun behind the books.

"That you?" I ask, nodding toward the paintings. "What happened to her, the little girl? All you showed is her fist."

"Don't know. I treat 'em. Then we move on. Or they go up on a Black Hawk. Never know what happens."

"And your sister," I say. He knows I mean the last picture.

He gets up. That's a place he's not going. But I think about her.

Later he says, "Like to meet your grandmother."

I say, "She's the one my mother says wants to cook Pilot."

"I'd like to meet her," he says.

HUT

When I take my mother to the doctor on Friday morning, I bring Pilot to Luke's cabin so she doesn't stay home with my grandmother, and Luke and Pilot can run on the beach. Luke is pacing. The cabin is eleven paces from the kitchen to the back door, plus four paces to circle the chair, six paces around the table. Repeat four times. The rustle of cellophane at the back door. The click of the lighter. The smell of the smoke. Luke's foot makes a jerky beat on the floor.

Silence. Study the early morning for movement.

Repeat.

Pilot has fallen into step with him. Luke knows. It slows him down. His face is stormy. "We're going to kill each other." He says this barely audibly.

"What do you mean?"

He leans down into my face. "I can't stand it. I can't stand my mind when I'm not working three days straight. I should go back."

"To your family?"

"To the war."

I think of the beautiful child he drew, his sister.

"If I went with you, could you go home? To your family."

"You'd drop out of school? I'd say, Hey, Ma, meet my girlfriend. Because of me, she's a runaway."

"Then you go."

"They don't know me," he shouts.

"Then call."

He slams the wall with his fist. "I can't take the nightmares."

The paint and wallboard crack.

I dream. A vision. Once more I remember the house where my mother screamed. I'm with her in her dream, a bamboo hut on stilts above the grass. We watch for the boy guard with the ax. I see Yiey's gentle lips as her eyes follow us. I see my mother's grandmother, through her eyes. There is almost nothing to her grandmother's body except for her enormous eyes.

"Sofie Grear," Luke whispers, maybe not to me. "Can you go? It's time. If you still can." He stops by the door. And when he does, Pilot rests her whole body at his feet.

I don't know what to say. I say, "My mother's waiting."

Pilot thinks we're leaving. She's by my side.

We are frozen, and I wonder if sorrow can make our hearts stop beating.

Outside, sun shines on the snow.

"Pilot," he whispers. She returns to Luke, licks his hand.

He doesn't look at me.

I say, "I won't be long."

I touch my dog's floppy ears. I say, "I'm coming back," to both of them. "I'm not leaving."

MY FRIEND

I go to school late, after the doctor, after I pick up Pilot. Pilot had made a nest of Luke's clothes on his bed, and the bed had a layer of sand. They had run, and then maybe Luke slept, pressed into Pilot's sleek back.

I see Rosa in class. "After school," she says. "Kilim." She wants to talk.

"I haven't used them," I say, feeling the ring in my pocket. She can guess."I'm not checking up," she says. "I miss you."

I shake my head, distracted. I carry the weight of the morning sadness and put it on my friend. I say, "Let's go to Kilim."

I need her to talk. I need Rosa to tell me about things we have always talked about. I ask, "How are things with the music industry?"

"I'm singing on Thursday night at the Press Room," Rosa says, her eyes narrowed on me.

"No kidding. You got hired?" I say.

"It's Beat Night. Anybody can read a poem. Mine's just to music. Will you come?"

"Sure," I say.

"You won't," she says. "You work on Thursdays. I know your life better than you do."

"I wish I could," I say. I miss her. But I'm wound so tight.

"I'm excited," Rosa says. "It's my big chance." She is half mocking herself and half earnest.

Rosa is treating us to hot chocolates. I watch her, attracted to all her colors. She is vibrant with yellow earrings and plaited hair coiled at the base of her neck and a short yellow skirt with black tights.

My Rosa. I feel a longing for her, when she's here, my friend. And I have moved to the far side of the moon.

A new girl behind the counter slowly spoons whipped cream over the hot chocolate. With the mug warming my hands, I make my way toward our regular spot, the window seat scattered with magazines. In the window seat I soak in the heat of the afternoon sun like a cat.

Rosa comes with her hot chocolate. I'm happy in that second to be with her, and I smile.

"There it is. Your knockout smile," she says.

From Rosa's dazzling yellows I look down to the mug. The girl at the counter has drawn the shape of a rabbit in the cream in the round white moon of the cup.

The rabbit's front legs are running, outstretched, his back legs float upwards, and his long ears fly back, etched in the brown of the chocolate. "Look," I say. "She made a rabbit." I show her my cup, but the rabbit is melting. It is dissolving into the moon.

"Cool," Rosa says. "She made me a bird."

But she is looking at me, not the bird or the rabbit.

"I'm worried about you."

I glance up.

"Are you fasting?"

"No," I say. "But this tastes like I have been. Like it's the first hot chocolate I've ever tasted."

I touch my finger to the cream, put a dot on my tongue. I

know things I don't know how to tell her. I can't tell her that this morning I wondered if Luke is right, that I need to go, that sometimes we scare each other.

Rosa's eyes are gleaming. "More news," she says. "They're going to interview me at the radio station, me and the other kids doing Beat Night. I am so nervous."

I laugh. This feels like old times. "Rosa Page on the radio."

"Should I go by just Page? Is that cooler? *Just call me Page.*"

"I'm jealous," I say.

She looks at her phone. "Twenty minutes. I play live. On the radio. Not just in my bedroom."

"You are perfect," I say.

And then, "What's going on with Luke?"

"He's on a scallop boat. And I'm researching a community supported fishery like that other boat out of Rye. I'm writing a business plan for economics."

Her eyes narrow on me. I've seen her mother's do that on her. "What aren't you saying?"

"What do you mean?"

She stares me down with those violet eyes.

"It's the opposite of what we did." I focus on the cup. "I'm following all the regs, this time. But it could still be a way for my dad to stay in the business."

"Sofie! It's me you're talking to. You disappeared. What's going on?"

Something lets go in me. I let my shoulders slide down the wall. I pull my cap over my eyebrows and look up at her. "I'm not sure what I'm doing," I tell Rosa. "I find him . . . why do I find him so magnetic?" I say.

She scrunches up her lips, thoughtful, as if she's supposed to have the answer.

"I don't know," she says. "I never felt like that about anybody."

"We listen so closely to each other."

Rosa watches me, waiting. Is she worried?

"He keeps reliving the war. Terrible nightmares. So he almost never sleeps."

There's missing information I still don't tell.

"Can you get out of this?" Rosa asks.

I let out a huge sigh. I rest the cup that warms my hands on the table.

"We could go out on Saturday night," she says. "Find somebody who's not an avalanche."

"I don't want to leave," I say. Both my hands are open to her as if Rosa has a potion, something to take my fear. Do something. "It's not just about wanting him. I do *want* him. But when he talks to me, I think, oh god stay, please stay, you help me understand my crazy self. Is that selfish?"

Rosa's phone goes off. She has to go. She stands. "Keep texting, okay? Tell me what's happening. There's help for soldiers. I see community college ads—*we are the most soldier-friendly school.*"

At the door she says, "Sounds to me like you're in love."

I let my hands fall.

CINNAMON

I decide not to see him on Saturday. On Sunday I text him.

"Meet me at Kilim," I text. Maybe I can make Luke be like regular people, make me be like regular people who wait here for their fathers to get home, hang out with their friends.

He comes. Like everybody, jacket collar pulled up around his neck, a stocking cap over his ears, hands shoved in his pockets. "Eleven degrees," I hear at the counter. Luke is eyeing others as he makes his way in. He has to check the hands in a crowded place, he had told me. Where are people's hands? What are they holding? Kilim is tight and small. He watches.

We order coffee, mine with extra room. Then we go to the counter where there are shakers of cinnamon and nutmeg and pitchers of cream and milk. We look at each other, catch each other's eyes from beneath all our clothes.

I say, "Hey, Luke."

He says, "Hey, Seal."

"Seal?"

"You're like a seal moving through the water. In my mind."

I try to laugh, and I fill my cup with milk and shake cinnamon, missing the cup, getting it all over the counter. "When you say that," I whisper to him, "it feels like sex."

He keeps his eyes down. But he says it again. "Seal."

This isn't working. This is nothing like being with my friends. We are gliding, slow motion, through the sea. We sit in the back at Kilim. I take off my cap, and my hair falls. We're knee to knee beneath Turkish carpets hanging from the walls and tucked in the scent of our coffee doused in cinnamon. All my life there's been a book at Kilim with threads that stitch the pages so loosely, whole sections fall away from the spine. It's by Rumi, and someone has left it on the table where we're sitting.

He reaches for me, his fingers on the flesh inside my wrist. Somehow I feel it to the cradle of my spine. We pull back in the din of voices in the café, crack up at ourselves, as if we weren't drowning. He opens the book on the table. "Had a friend over there who read Rumi. Took it with him on patrol."

He presses the frayed spine to the table and turns the book so that we can both read. On one page, Luke drops his finger to a line. *What hurts you blesses you.*

Is this what praying is? Cinnamon in our coffee, in our hair; deep-red Turkish carpets; the clink of cups; threads that hold a spine.

I'll stay a little while.

TAPS

Luke comes for dinner to little Cambodia to meet my grandmother and my mother and see where we all have regular, small fights at the top of our voices.

Maybe we are all grateful when he walks in, all five foot ten of him towering over both of them. He smells like the sea and woodsmoke. I want to wrap both of my legs around him and pull him down on the couch. Who knows what my mother would say about that?

He is polite, but straight-lipped, shyly stern. He has parted his dark hair carefully and combed it flat down to his ears. It's still a little damp. Yiey puts bowls of rice and green curry on the table. She and my mother have been snapping at each other as they chopped. There is so much rage in their fingers that hold the chopping knives I think the rage must infiltrate the red peppers and we will all begin shouting after the first mouthful. But the food also surprises me with its colors and beauty.

My mother brings more. She brings chaquai, the long fried bread, warm from the oven, and jackfruit and slices of golden mango she must have bought at the Asian market by my Dunkin' Donuts.

"You're a fisherman too," my mother says to Luke.

"I'm a soldier," he says.

I look at him, alarmed. I look at his hands, wound tight in a ball. Pilot places her nose on top of his knotted hands. He does not look at me.

"When she was little—" my mother says, pointing at me.

I say, "How would you know about when I was little? You weren't there."

"When she was little," she says, "I used to change the sheets at the Ashworth Hotel, me and the Irish girls. They got visas for the summer. And this one . . ." She jabs her finger at me again. "She followed her father up and down the fishing pier at Rye Harbor. She had red rubber boots."

"I did not," I say, vaguely remembering tiny red rubber boots in the attic.

"I bought you pink dresses," she accuses. "I got her a stuffed bunny in a pink apron and baby dolls that cried. Do you think she would wear a pink dress?" my mother asks Luke.

Luke says, "She wears a lot of olive drab and boots."

My mother shakes her head. "Never," she says. "Stubborn girl."

Yiey tells him about fishing in Cambodia. Catfish, she says. "And in the river here," she says. "If you go at right time, they play songs from the river."

"She means from the shipyard," I say. "They play it on the sound system, and the fishermen on Peirce Island can hear. Some song with bugles at sunset. Taps?"

"It's not Taps," Luke says. "A bugler plays Taps at a funeral. More likely it's Retreat."

"Maybe it Tap," Yiey says. I know she likes funerals. She had said they often didn't get to bury people in the war. "What is Tap?" Yiey says.

Luke clears his throat. He gazes outside, out the window nearly covered with windblown snow. He begins to whistle Taps for her. He becomes the Lucas Sanna I don't know. His whistling is darkly gorgeous. He walks to the window. He holds the notes, and the sound sends chills through me.

We are still as we listen.

"Yes," she says. "That is where I fish. Off the rocks and maybe they play Tap. The wind blow it across the water. It a sad song."

Luke clears his throat again. Maybe he forgot we were there. His hands hang by his side.

"My husband, soldier kill him," Yiey says. I am aware that she uses the present tense when she talks. It makes it seem like the killing is now, in the present. Right now the soldiers are wrestling her husband to the ground; the first sound blasts.

Luke looks at the ice on the window. "I'm sorry," he says, so softly we can barely hear him. Our conversation is painful. We have vast silences, but it is better than the haranguing. My mother rubs her hands down her belly, "Aghhhh," she moans and digs her heels into the rug laced with tiny black dog hairs.

"You're not going to have that baby now?" Luke teases my mother.

The women gaze at him.

"I was a medic," he says, "but I'd just as soon not handle this."

Pilot eyes the hot dishes of beautiful, spiteful food. We eat, and for a few minutes we don't have to talk. Yiey pulls the gold locket she wears from her shirt. She opens the locket and shows Luke the photo inside.

I know it is a tiny picture of my grandfather.

"My husband," she says.

Luke nods.

"You a soldier," she says. "Who do you kill?" Still present tense.

"Anyone," Luke says. "They arm the medics. But if we fire it's a last resort."

My mother has eaten for two. My grandmother's plate is empty. We are sitting around the coffee table. A bowl with remaining egg rolls and a bowl a quarter full of rice are on the coffee table. All the other food is eaten.

"Did you have food to eat?" Yiey asks Luke. My mother eats more rice.

"Food in plastic," he says. "We weren't hungry."

But I am thinking of the gun. *Who do you kill?* my grandmother asks.

"When I come to this country," Yiey says. "I lay in bed. I cannot move. I cannot sleep. I feel hands around my neck to kill me. They get me around my neck and I cannot breathe. At Lowell General, they say I am crazy. Nothing wrong. Five times I almost pass away when the hands squeeze my neck."

I have no memory of this story. I have a shadow of a memory of my bed in Lowell.

Maybe we all slept in that bed, like the children in Cambodia. My mother doesn't tell stories. She inches down on the couch; her head rests on her mother's shoulder.

"You aren't crazy," Luke says. "I'm in the war every second of my life. Those hands around my throat."

I say, "He dreams about someone."

"Who?" she speaks sharply. She demands to know, as if she knows all the ghosts and maybe this one is hers, too.

I don't know if he'll answer, but it feels good to me to take his nightmare out of the dark night in the cabin and bring it to Yiey.

His voice shakes, but he answers her. He tells her the story he told me. The dream of trying again to save a soldier. "He dies again. Every night. Then they get me. I think that's saying, you weren't meant to come back. Just the ghost of me came back."

My mother has fallen asleep. My phone chimes—a text from my father. He's fishing in the morning.

My grandmother says, "Sophea, she should not be with a ghost."

I can tell my grandmother likes him, but that does not stop her from scolding. I want to tell her, *Stop it! He's fine*, but they aren't talking to me.

"No." Luke agrees. "She shouldn't be." His face is drained of feeling.

It's as if I'm not here. They've become allies.

“What did you do to be able to sleep?” Luke asks my grandmother.

“Go to monk,” she says. “The monk help me. I have to go eight time.”

“Eight,” Luke says, as if this number is magic and he must remember.

“Eight time,” she says. “In Lowell is the monk.”

Luke says, “And after eight times, you slept?”

“I do no pass away.”

I leave them and go to the window. My grandmother brings me my plate of food. “Sophea,” she commands. “Eat.”

READING KEROUAC

I'm reading Kerouac to understand Luke. He's cooking shrimp to understand me. In my imagination, Luke is Kerouac as a boy—he flies down a field, hooks a football on an orange fall night.

"Are you hungry?" Luke calls as he spins the shrimp in butter and garlic in a cottage in Rye. I wander the streets in Lowell with a boy in love. First my name is Maggie. Then I am a Cambodian girl, and we squat on the floor of a triple decker, spooning rice and shrimp in our mouths, and the moon is full.

When he talks to someone I don't know on the phone, Luke is Kerouac in war. He falls into a voice I don't know.

I imagine him as a soldier in the movies, crouched outside a door, gun ready, his eye to the gun sight. Or he is giving chocolate to kids. Dozens of arms are reaching up to him to get the chocolate. Anyone could have a grenade; anyone can be the enemy.

UNPROTECTED

I'm doing my homework, and Luke stretches out in the chair. I am stuffed with shrimp and rice. I hear the bell buoy sound. I look up from my small light and see him as a shadow. I think he is finally sleeping. I see him in gray profile. First his long nose, the square tension of his jaw, the soft tissue I know is around his ear.

I imagine the tiny curls of hair where his ribs curve below his heart. His chest is not protected. I watch it lift. The ribs expand. What if I placed my palms on the exposed fleshy part of his arms? The part no one touches. Not even the wind. Then I let my eyes roam the shape of his chin, his cheeks now more visible as my eyes adjust. Hard jaw. The sockets of his eyes.

His eyes. For the first time since I met him, for a second I'm afraid. He's not asleep. His eyes are fixed, open. They watch the door with the concentration, the tremor of an animal.

A gull screams. Now I listen with him. I see all that can harm us.

The clock—its ticks.

The cottage's electric hum.

From the breakwater, the foghorn.

His shoulders drop, grip the bed. His spine arches.

If I startled him, would he forget for a second who we are?

CAMBODIAN

"You say you aren't Cambodian," Luke says the next time we meet.

"No, I'm not Cambodian," I say.

I have cut three branches of winter berries I found behind the horseshoe of cabins near Rye harbor. I place the branches in a jar. Beside the jar I place a tin of sand, and in the sand three sticks of incense.

In the dark I light the incense. The scent of jasmine settles on us.

"There," I say. "Maybe we will be safe."

"You made a shrine," he says, "like your grandmother does."

I look at my hands that collected the branches. One rests in the other.

JAM

The incense burns. I am almost Luke's lover. We live in a cabin near the ocean, where seals will soon have pups and sun themselves on the breakwater, and I cook rice for us and sometimes we lie together in each other's arms until 9:00 p.m.

Tonight when it's time to go, he makes me coffee. He puts in three sugars and three fingers of milk. He makes toast to warm me and slathers my toast with bright raspberry jam. It makes me feel childlike and in love.

"Stay warm," he says.

I'm also the schoolgirl who gets out of bed for my shift on Saturday in a Cambodian house. I imagine him kicking up the fire in the woodstove. I make coffee with hot milk and sugar the way he does for me, and I drink.

I drive to work.

In the parking lot, I call my father. I'd give anything to hear his voice.

"It's my girl," he calls into the phone.

"Dad, what are you doing?"

"Gonna lose the call. The signal won't hold."

"Just wanted to hear your—"

I hear him faintly. ". . . try to make it home . . ." I hear. ". . . don't know."

"Are you coming?" It is almost my birthday. But I hear only silence. He's somewhere offshore, in the Atlantic Ocean. I need to stop calling. It only hurts when it's done.

The trees still bend to each other, weighted with snow. The plows have scraped snow from the streets, yet ice caps on piles of snow remain like scar tissue.

But I love the color of the jam Luke gives me on toast. It brightens all this long February.

WHY THEY DON'T SPEAK FRENCH

My mother and Yiey sit by the woodstove. I am upstairs after work, but I can hear them. I'm working on my business plan for a CSF. I'm writing lists in my computer and sketching notes and fish on a brown paper bag. Monkfish, cod, hake, dogfish. To do:

1. Inspection. A jamoke from the state boards your boat and your truck, and looks at all your stuff.
2. Teach customers how to shuck, fillet, eviscerate, process, and freeze so they don't get sick and sue you.
3. Sole proprietor. How to do it? File for insurance. Prove how you won't make people sick with your fish.
4. Get federal permit to harvest and land, federal dealer's permit, state permit to sell to shareholders in a CSF, forms for estimated taxes and other fed tax forms, mobile vendor license from the city so you can go to the farmer's market.

"What are you doing?" my mother shouts.

"A business plan for homework," I shout.

"My grandfather had a business," she shouts.

I imagine a fishmonger dragging eels, gasping for breath, on a cart.

"In Paris," she shouts. "Where he studied."

My eyes pause, as I hear this, on the hake fins I am shading, overwhelmed with the paperwork to sell the fish you catch, the rules, the government that thinks it is god.

"A banker," Yiey shouts. "At home speak French. Pa say in France, you lucky, you learn French and Khmer."

"You lived in France?" I shout.

"Until I am five," she shouts.

"But if the Khmer Rouge hear you speak French, they beat you till you die. She never hear a whisper of French," my grandmother shouts. She must be talking about my mother.

"Here, you can be clever, like a rabbit," my mother shouts. "You can have a business. If you can keep your mind from Cambodia."

I imagine them downstairs, sitting side by side. My grandmother with a scarf tied over her thin hair. And beautiful Lydia, my mother, her black hair fashioned in spirals she made with a curling iron, wearing a polka-dot dress. She shouts, "He hiccupped. See!" and I imagine one of the red dots flick in her red silky dress.

Who am I?

I come from a fisherman, a hunter of crickets, and now from a family of bankers in France.

CALLING THE SOULS

I lie down to sleep in my low bed in the upstairs room by the window that my father cut into the side of the roof. In winter, standing on tiptoe, I can see the river at daybreak. And on a clear night I can see the sky. Tonight the moon is lopsided, on the way to becoming whole. I imagine my father's finger drawing the line of the letter *P* as he points to the long side of the moon, and his voice, *See the P.* I hear his voice especially tonight because he said he'd try to come home for my birthday, tomorrow.

He'd come if there were bad prospects for fishing. If a cat crossed his path, or the moon had a halo.

"Call doctor! Call doctor!" It's my grandmother. Pilot lifts her ears. I shut my eyes. I dig deeper into my bed. What is the matter with my mother now? She's prone to hysterics. I wonder what Luke is doing this moment? My belly feels hollow. I think of his hand on my belly.

"Sophea, call doctor!" Yiey is climbing the stairs to my loft, calling, "Sophea."

I slide into the cold from my bed. "What's the matter?"

"Srey Pov! It's Srey Pov." My mother's Cambodian nickname. Little sister.

I come to their bedroom where they sleep with all their clothes and new outfits for the baby and herb plants to protect them in winter. My mother's eyes are open, but she doesn't talk. Sometimes she closes her eyes. Then she screams that she can't breathe and she clutches her heart.

"Mom, get up. Come on, I'll make you hot chocolate." She drinks tons of hot chocolate. But my mother's eyes glaze over.

"Should we go to the emergency room?" I say. Her eyes scare me. "Mom. Let's get you in a coat. It's barely twelve degrees."

"No!" Yiey has my cell phone to my ear. "Doctor! Soldier."

I turn to look at her frantic black eyes.

"The hospital does not understand *neak-ta*," she says.

"I don't either," I say. "What is neak-ta?"

"Wandering spirit," she says. "You have to call them back to the body. The ghosts of the murdered people want call them away. The doctor, he understand," she says. "The ghost want the baby."

My mother is breathing fast and very shallow. She lifts her hands to her throat.

My grandmother says, "Her heart going to stop. The air can't come inside."

My grandmother presses her hands on my mother's chest where her heart is. Her eyes are wide with terror.

I text Luke, *Can you come. Emergency.*

Luke wears a heavy camouflage jacket and looks bear-sized in my mother's room.

She is tiny except for her belly that is covered with a bright silk cloth embroidered with mangoes and other fruit I don't know. He leans down and puts an ear to her heart. I see his wide knuckles as he places his fingers on my mother's tiny wrist and listens to her pulse. He doesn't have anything but his hands. In Afghanistan, he would have worn that fifty-pound first aid kit hitched to his back. I remember the painting of a dressing that hooked over a chest and a long, long tail to wrap around and stop the blood.

He says, "Do you feel hot and sweaty?"

My mother shakes her head.

"Where does it hurt?"

"Here," she says, gasping, and places her hand on top of her chest, just beneath the breastbone where Yiey's hands had been.

"Didn't feel pain down to here?" He touches her extended left arm.

"No, here." She places both hands on her heart. "I am suffocating." She is still panting. "My brain is spinning," she says. "I stood, and all my blood flew to my head."

"Doesn't look like a heart attack," Luke says, "Do you have vertigo?"

"Yes," she says.

"When you stand, you're dizzy?"

"I am a hurricane. I am going to die. The baby will die too."

He doesn't respond to this. He tells her to stretch out.

"Why should I?" she says.

"To loosen up," he says.

She scowls at him but tries to untwist herself, release her back, supporting her belly, down the length of the bed where she had rolled into a knot. But she tenses and lifts.

"It's coming back. They are killing us."

Luke places his hand on the bed beside her forehead.

"We're gonna breathe. That's all we're gonna do. Breathe with me."

She cries out. "I can't. I told you."

"Inhale," he says. But she is arched and gasping. "That's it," he says. He keeps praising her. "You got it." And he counts very slowly, "Two, three, four. That's it, hold on with me." Even though she's not breathing with him, he keeps counting. "Try it if you like. If you want to see what it feels like. It's called ratio breath. Might help. It might not."

He counts, "Exhale . . . two . . . three . . . four . . ."

Yiey shouts, "He doctor, do it!"

"Inhale . . . two . . . three . . . four . . ."

Her breath is jagged, and she gulps air to his count.

"Exhale . . . two . . . three . . . four . . ."

My mother's breath gradually slows. She begins to breathe with Luke to his rhythm.

"Trick they taught us before they discharged us. Old PTSD trick. Don't think about shit. Just count to four with each breath."

"Keep counting," my mother demands.

"Exhale . . . two . . . three . . . four . . . maybe you can go to five."

I see her shoulders begin to release into the blanket beneath her. Luke counts to inhale. Two. Three. Four. Then counts to five when they breathe out. She breathes with her hands rising on her enormous belly until she lets go, into sleep. Luke doesn't have a clue that he needs what he just gave my mother.

"Good," Yiey says. "The spirit back."

She holds a match to the sticks of incense in a jar. A thick floral scent fills all the spaces of the bedroom. "This we burn with monk," she says. "When monk give blessing."

I try to imagine what it would be like to have your spirit separate from your body. Luke is on his knees on the floor; his arm rests on a small yellow blow-up tub to bathe the new baby. His eyelids keep trying to close. Maybe we each have our souls for a little while and we can sleep.

When the house is settled, I take Luke's hand. He is nearly falling asleep like my mother has. I'm asking him to stay.

He shakes his head.

"They're asleep," I whisper. "You'd fall asleep in the car."

I lead him up the stairs to my bed. I catch glimpses of him in the moonlight in my room. How strange to see the back of his head, the muscles of his neck, the outline of his dark hair here in my tiny room. We shiver together under my covers, warming each other in the cold house.

"Happy birthday, Sofie Grear," he says into my hair. "Wish to hell I'd met you before." He speaks in a voice so low some words crack or fall away. "Or after. Long time. Seven years after." I feel his breath on my neck as he whispers.

"I'll be twenty-four," I whisper.

"Eight times," I think he says. His breath is slow, even. I can't see his eyes, but I know they have closed.

Four counts to breathe in.

Five counts to breathe out.

Eight times you go to the monk so you don't pass away.

I wake before dawn. In sleep, Luke and I are all crossed arms and crossed legs.

"Luke," I warn him. "Luke," I whisper again. He lifts. I slide from the bed but stop at the door. On my bureau, in the streak of light from my small lamp, is the gun. Even coming here, he is armed with the gun. Does he need the gun to feel whole? It gives me a chill to see the pistol on my bureau beside my whelk shell and my silver hairbrush.

Suddenly I remember my father. Jesus! What if my father had come? What if he drove all night and slipped in in the dark of the early morning? I carefully call out Luke's name before I approach the bed. He has warned me to do this.

"Luke, go," I say. "You need to go." He remembers my father is coming too, and he hustles into his jacket in the cold dark.

I go downstairs first. My father is not asleep on the couch. No extra car in the driveway. My father said if he came, he'd borrow the car of a guy on his crew. Luke comes behind me.

At the front door I whisper, "Don't turn your headlights on." I am so cold. He presses his warm body to mine, and he is a fire to me even in the winter wind.

He steps into the dark.

He pulls his dark car away from the curb and into the street.

I let Pilot out, and when I come in, I see the flash of color of Yiey's wrap she wears at night. I see it in the light of the bathroom just before she shuts the door.

I wait to bring Pilot in.

When I get my dog and I silently shut the door, both Yiey and my mother stand together, blocking my way. "You cannot see him again," my mother says.

I look at her, speechless at first. A few hours ago she couldn't breathe and Yiey had called Luke and he had come for her.

"I don't believe you said that," I whisper. "Never talk to me that way. When I was a child I would have done anything for you."

"He is no good for you," Yiey says.

"Who are you to tell me I can't see him?" I shove past them. "You can't tell me. You are nothing to me. My father let you stay in my house. That is all we are to each other."

"I know that boy," she says. "He got lost with the ghosts. A ghost can't love you."

I hold on to the railings and lean into her. "If you say one more thing I am leaving." All this comes out in one low breath not well thought out. "I'll pack up my clothes and my dog and you'll never see me again. I'm counting the days till my father comes back. Sixty days. Then we're done."

Just then my phone beeps. I glance down, thinking Luke. But it's my father. *On my way*, he writes. My father. He's coming. And they are going to tell him.

Of all things, Yiey comes to me on the stairs. She brings her hands to my face. I see her eyes that now seem to hold my rage in her pain. I burst into tears.

I do *not* want to feel affection for her. The affection that I feel.

In my bedroom, I see the gun is gone.

BIRTHDAY

My father slides into Atlantic Heights at sunset. He drove all day for my birthday.

He enters with an enormous grin, a beard, his cap for me that says *Mason Oil Co., Inc., Chincoteague, Va.*, and a cake the size of the Gulf of Maine.

The cake says *Happy Birthday, Sofie* and has a porcelain dog in the middle with white feet and floppy ears. "Couldn't get you a dog again, so I got you a cake with a dog. Looked all over the tourist shops for that dog." Pilot came last birthday, a month late, while we waited for the dog rescue van to make its way from Georgia to the parking lot of the New Hampshire State Liquor Store.

My father says, "Call Rosa." He is determined to make this a party.

Rosa comes, smiling and luminous. She hugs my father. She hugs my mother and grandmother, who take in her tiny short skirt and the hoops in her ears. She brings me a huge bouquet of daffodils. I hold them like a torch, waiting for something awful to happen.

"Oh, food, I am starving," she says to my grandmother, who is stirring green curry at the stove. Then six of us sit around the woodstove: Dad, my mother, Yiey, Rosa, and me, and Pilot who could have been cooked by now, herself. And in my mind are also

Rithy (who caught crickets), and Yiey's mother, and Luke. I do not look at my mother or Yiey. We have not spoken since Luke's escape. We will never speak again.

My father wants everybody to be happy. He's got about twenty minutes to make it happen since he has to head back to Chincoteague at dawn and his eyelids are heavy.

After the curry, he asks, "You got a wish?" as he lights the candles on the cake.

"Yes, I have my wish." I look at no one. I blow out seventeen candles, and my father cuts the cake into enormous pieces of white cake streaked with chocolate—a thunder-and-lightning cake with chocolate frosting. The frosting is slightly hardened from the trip but sweet and eventually melts on our tongues.

"February twentieth," he says. "Soon it'll be March, and I'm home in the spring. How's it going up here?"

No one answers, we are so full of secrets. We nod our heads, letting the frosting melt in our mouths.

"What's new?" he says.

I wait. Here's their chance.

But my mother doesn't begin, not even with telling him about her soul wandering and who came to bring it back. Rosa does not tell him she gave me her supply of condoms as she did not currently need them, but I must replace them.

Finally Yiey asks him, "How is fish in Chincoteague?"

What is going on? I wonder.

"Abundant," he says, nodding as well. "Good season. Paying the boat. Paying the fuel. And this."

He pulls a box out from under his chair. I take the top off the box, and whatever is inside is wrapped in old nautical maps, which he knows I love. When I was little I studied them and traced my finger over Jeffrey's Ledge, all the ledges, all the places he said the fish swim in schools. I spread open the maps.

Inside them is a dress. It's yellow. I've never worn anything yellow. It has satin straps and looks like something to wear to a ball. I don't know what to make of it, so I go and put it on. I think it belongs to Virginia of the Old South, but I keep it on. I also put on the *Mason Oil Co., Inc. Chincoteague, Va.* baseball cap. Then go and sit on the floor between Rosa's feet. Pilot has eaten, so she drops on the floor and stretches her long legs, pressing her back into me.

There is so much deliberate not-speaking between the Cambodians and me. It's hard to cut through it. My mother and Rosa talk about how to curl hair that naturally hangs black, shiny, and straight. Above our heads, Luke and I were together last night, imagining what if we'd met seven years from today.

My father sees the shrine in the corner. He sees my mother finding no easy way to be still on the couch. I wonder if he remembers when they were young and she was pregnant with me and he knew the sweet and sharp smell of the incense she burned. Or if he is just worried about the Bong guy in Lowell and wants her to be safe, maybe even find some happiness.

"What did you see in the sea?" Rosa tries. "When we were little—do you remember? You said there was a stop in the sea where you could fill up with fuel and get beer? I believed it and ever since thought there were little stops out there in the sea for snacks."

"No stops in this sea," he says. "I've seen the wind. You can't trust it. This wind sweet-talks you. Calls you out on the deck. Invites you to pull up the earflaps, take in the stillness. And you do. Invites you to settle in, might as well check to see if you got reception. The wind lets you talk to your kid.

"When the wind's got you where it wants you," my father goes on, "it rips off the hull. Makes you pray to god you paid the insurance."

I have a flash of a thought. Had my mother been lonely with Dad? Did she ever sleep with his shirt the way I used to, because it smelled like his skin? Wear his cap, like I do now on my seventeenth birthday?

My father's face turns stern. "Something sure as the stars is going on here. Just don't kill each other before I get back," he says.

I feel my grandmother's eyes on me. They don't scare me. It's like we have a feminine presence with us after all these years of hardscrabble love and the determined hunch of my father's shoulders while he put a meal together for me day after day.

My grandmother's eyes observe, seem to say, *There's no end of things love can call for.*

I beg my father, "Dad, please stay."

"You know I can't, Sofie girl."

I wrap my arms around his neck. His scratchy shirt scrapes my cheek.

"Seventeen," he says in disbelief. I feel him swallow like he does when emotion's got him by the throat.

"Please stay."

JOY

"Come for a minute," Luke says.

I have my dog. I bring her whenever I can, just in case. She's curled by the woodstove.

Luke says, "Here." Toward the bed. A tiny smile.

I feel his hand on my neck. At the same time, I hear the sound of snowplows on the road trying to keep up with the snow. I hear a bell buoy. I hear a melody that I have heard sometime in my life, and I hear the words of the title but I don't know what they mean. Pka Proheam Rik Popreay.

In his bed, I try to keep my eyes on the alarm clock. But we disappear. He touches my cheek. I lean into him. "Oh," he whispers. "Oh." I close my eyes. His palm presses a line from my cheekbone down to my jaw. I have never felt anything as charged as my jaw in this second. It becomes the total focus of my body. He traces my lips. I feel my body release. I see a small trace of moonlight enter the cottage window. His hands run down my legs still in snow pants against the cold. His hand is hard and sweet and hungry. I laugh because I have on my snow pants. I unzip them and slide my legs out of them and Luke covers my legs with his.

He draws my hair back from my face and smiles at my laughing.

"Just to touch you," he says.

I have no words to answer. I can only nod, yes.

He takes off my layers, piece by piece. I watch his face. I say, "We are really doing this."

He says, "We are really."

I help him undress, feeling his heat.

Under the covers, I take his hand in my two and we are drunk with joy. Surprising out-of-nowhere joy. It is like we have found this beautiful oasis while the moonlight fills the window and the buoy sounds, and the ocean is just an ocean. It's not calling me or haunting. I run my hand over his, then bring his palm to my mouth and kiss him. I laugh again. Even a palm sends a charge through my body. I kiss his neck. He pulls me back to look at my face. His expression has become serious and searching. He draws my body to his. We feel our bodies hip bone to hip bone. We don't talk. We float in this place of moonlight and touch.

We kiss for years. Years pass while I place my hand on his chest and his thighs.

I lie on him, feeling him, while we kiss. "Just imagine," I laugh. He laughs. For a few years we are ecstatic, joyous children over what we have just discovered. The joy of our simple bodies.

We are on our backs looking at the knots in the ceiling. They are gorgeous knots.

"I was just letting my mind run," I whisper.

"Where?" he says.

"What are you doing this summer?"

"I live a day at a time."

"We are making a string of days," I say.

I roll into him and I'm laughing again. "This is our house. We'll paint the whole place . . . what color?"

"Grecian green."

"Grecian green," I agree. "Then we'll raise seven or so kids."

"This summer?" he says.

"And go someplace warm."

"How about Savannah?" he says.

"Okay," I say, "Savannah. We'll get in the car and just keep on driving. Till the ice falls away and the blacktop shows. And the forsythia's blooming."

"Okay," he says.

"We can do anything," I say. "What else would you want? If you could have anything."

"Stop by Jeannotte's Market in Nashua. I used to get subs there when I was a kid. I lived around the corner."

He holds me and presses his lips into my throat, a bridge of kisses across my collarbone.

He whispers, "I want to sleep. Do people sleep in Savannah? We're outta here, girl."

This is all possible even though in the background I remember like a song—eleven paces kitchen to the back door, plus four to circle the chair, six around the table, repeat four times, the rustle of cellophane at the door, the click of the lighter, the smell of the smoke, repeat until . . .

WHAT YOU SAVE

I refuse to talk to my mother even after she did not betray me to my father. But late Sunday morning I'm alone in the house, and I take over her and my grandmother's room like it's mine. I drag the rocking chair in there and eat while I rock and glare at the photos on the wall and prowl through their stuff.

A Cambodian man is on the wall who is no more than twenty. He wears a suit jacket and has a good-looking, smiling face. Her father. My grandmother's husband. I guess he's my grandfather.

My mother tacked a length of fabric over the bed. She can't sleep unless a veil falls down around her. I study a postcard photo of the temple Angkor Wat. On the bedside table is brightly colored paper, gold and red, intricately folded with its corners tucked in. I try to open it. She will know if I can't replace these intricate folds. But I untuck each corner folded like an origami letter. Inside, the words are in Khmer. I trace my fingers over them. Then draw back, burned. Did I touch a swollen belly? A husband's love letter he wrote the day the soldiers took him? Is this how girls fold letters in Cambodia?

I see a blue urn in the room. A baby swing. I wind it up, and the swing glides back and forth across the bed. I know this song it plays while it swings. "If you go down in the woods today, you're in for a big surprise." "Teddy Bears Picnic." This was mine. My mother played it for me.

Finally a Buddha. She says she is okay when "a Buddha sleeps with me."

My mother comes home and catches me in there, but I don't care. I just keep rocking. I keep slurping chicken soup from a cup and wipe splatters of soup from my cheek onto the heel of my hand. She makes hot chocolate and comes back. She composes a birth announcement out loud for the upcoming birth while she looks at the man on the wall:

"Lydia Sun had a baby boy named Heng—means 'lucky'—maybe March 6, his grandfather's birthday, at Portsmouth Hospital, how, by section because his sister was born by section so Heng has to be too. His grandfather died in the Pol Pot time by execution. Heng is the son of Lydia Sun, born Phnom Penh, Cambodia, now of Portsmouth, New Hampshire."

ICE

In the afternoon, my mother leaves to walk in the woods on snow paths packed down by snowshoers and cross-country skiers. She wants to gather greens for Yiey's shrine for Observance Day of the new moon. She and Yiey have been to see a monk and hired him to come to do a blessing for the baby when the time comes.

Yiey urges me, "Just walk behind. Make sure she okay."

The paths crisscross the snow. It's one of those perfect winter days when the air is just warm enough so your fingers don't ache. You don't have to cover your nose and cheeks from the burn of the cold. The sun shines down, and after all these days of snow, it looks like a winter thaw. Pilot races the length of the woods from the road to the river and back again.

"Just some red berries," my mother had called.

I don't pay attention. I'm counting days till this is over like soldiers in war. Tomorrow is a vacation day, and then I'm free to go to Luke's. I plotted it out. Work. Overnight with Rosa, I tell them. Tomorrow Luke and I will have all night. I dream, what if we could actually get in Luke's car and drive south, keep driving south till we come to Savannah. And have jam on toast in the mornings.

I see red berries on a snow-covered drooping branch. They hang heavy with winter wear. Pilot races up the riverbank, down to the river the length of the beach. It is low tide. Herring gulls hang out on the pier, raucous, waiting for a human and a little trash. Pilot on their trail. She chases them from pier to beach, running and running. But something ominous is happening on this sunny winter afternoon where the sun has begun to warm long-frozen edges of the river.

Although the Piscataqua is a fast-moving river, sometimes in a winter so bone-aching cold, room-sized ice chunks break off from the coves and wedge in the curves of the river. These floes are a big problem for fishermen, who have to avoid slamming their boats into any that break away and scream out to sea with the current. What if a rescue bird dog like Pilot, the tracking instinct deep in her blood, discovers she could track the birds farther out on the river than she has been able to track them all her life? Her temptation.

But a dog, my father had always said, is no match for this river.

Now I look out. My fist is full of drooping branches bearing thin, red berries. There is my dog, her right forepaw lifted, tail straight out, absolutely still. She is already out on a frozen chunk of the river as she holds this pose. From her stance I know, even from my distance, she trembles with focus and unbearable excitement.

When she bolts from her alert, the ice could move out and be taken by the rushing water. She would be swept into the current of the river at a temperature too cold to survive.

I race through the woods, along the cyclone fence, toward the river with the I-95 traffic flying overhead on the Piscataqua River Bridge to the beach and mudflats turned to ice where the gulls taunt my dog. They pose at the end of the pier and then all lift their wings and descend on a morsel I don't see on the ice.

Here is my mother, in her white coat and black hair, grasping winter greens for the shrine, but her eyes are on my dog. Pilot turns toward the gulls. From a statue, she transforms into a bird dog in flight on the trail of the screeching gulls. I hear the sound of the ice. It groans under Pilot as she grips for her footing, slipping, scrambling. I scream at her, "Come! Come now!"

This happens in seconds—something extraordinary. Something I don't think to do. My only thought, I am on the edge of the river, about to go out on the ice—on water! The thing I am most afraid of. I am driven by the picture of Pilot swept away in the current under the massive bridge and out to sea.

I take a step on the ice toward my dog. But my mother puts out her hand. "Wait," she calls.

"I can't," I scream. "She'll die."

But my mother too is transformed. She is composed, like Yiey. Like Luke. I hear the ice crack. She moves toward the steel framework of the pier. Now, at low tide, a person can walk halfway out the long pilings. She begins to walk through mudflats and then into the water. I see her slip. She grabs the metal frame for support. "Where are you going?" I shout. She can barely walk on the flat living-room floor. Pilot barks at the gulls. At the end, at what used to be a loading pier, hanging at an angle as if barely connected after all these years, is a ladder. She lifts her arms high, grabs ahold of the ladder, disengages it from what held it dangling over the water and half-formed ice. Then she turns back, dragging the ladder.

She is coming through the frozen mud and muck, breaking through ice. This is a woman who lies on her back and moans. I am awed. On the beach we drop the ladder, then push it slowly out onto the ice. She is clever to know what my father has said about a rescue on ice—you have to distribute your weight over as much space as you can.

"Now," she says. "On your belly." She places her hands on her own belly, and I believe she would have gone herself if it weren't for the baby. The ladder reaches almost to Pilot, who is frantic. I get down on all fours, then crawl out on the ladder until I am on my belly. I hear the ice crack. Just ahead a fissure shifts, opening under Pilot's weight. I am terrified. My mother holds the bottom of the ladder and in that way holds me.

"This way, Pilot," I call. *Keep the panic from your voice.* "Come, girl." My body is numb against the ice. My ice could break off, too, and become a floe. But my mother holds me. Just as I can almost touch her paw, Pilot gets her footing. I need her to jump. She's just three feet past me. Her haunches grip the ice.

Moving as gently as possible, I pull my scarf over my head, tie the tails in a knot. "Mom, push, one more foot." Pilot is crying as space grows between us.

My mother slides the ladder. I'm one foot closer. I toss the scarf, aiming to wrap it around her head and neck. She ducks, slipping on the ice, and I miss. Again.

Finally the ring of the scarf wraps around her neck. I pull. She leans down into the scarf. Her paws scramble, and then she leaps like a horse from the moving floe onto my peninsula of ice. It holds. We don't crash into the river. I wrap the scarf tight around her and hold her to my chest on the ladder. My mother pulls us back to the beach. Gingerly, we crawl the length of the ladder back to the sand.

I unknot the wet scarf from my dog. My mother takes off her white coat she always wears.

"You don't even like her," I say.

She is on the ground with Pilot. Her boots are ruined. Her coat is ruined. She places her muddy white coat on Pilot and wraps her body around my dog's shivering body.

"You do," she says. "I saved her for you."

HEARTBEAT

We make it home, my mother, Pilot, and I, smeared in seawater and mud, dragging red berries for Yiey so she can fix up the shrine.

The next morning my grandmother puts a bowl of rice with fish sauce in my hands. She gives me a fork. The peppers in the fish sauce make my nose flare. I bring the fork to my mouth. I taste this bite. I swallow.

"You eat this all the time when you are small," my grandmother says about the rice and pepper sauce.

They gave my mother a new appointment today, because they want to watch her. So this afternoon I will take my mother to the doctor. This morning, my grandmother and mother talk about disgusting things, cervixes dilating, constipation, Cesarean sections.

"It won't take long, will it?" I say. "I need to hurry."

"You said you would stay with me," she says.

"I am," I whine. "Aren't I here?" But I study her. I look at her wide eyes and wonder, ever since we collected the red berries.

At the doctor's office, I go in with my mother. If she tells the doctor that the baby is a ghost or any crazy Cambodian thing, I can try to bring it back to science, a subject I'm good at. What is real? What is happening? That is what I will tell the doctor.

I also want to hear what the doctor says. Dr. Sharma is dark-skinned, maybe from India or Nepal. No, she says she is from Bhutan. She wears two dozen or more bangles around her wrist.

My mother says to her, "This is my daughter, Sophea." A new tone is in her voice, the way she says my name. I have not heard this tone.

Dr. Sharma shakes my hand. "So tall. And now you will have a brother." She confuses me. Is she talking to me, the fisherman's kid? I'm lost in this body I'm in.

My mother lies on the examination table, and now I want to leave since this seems very personal, to see my mother's round, brown belly exposed. The doctor's fingertips work their way across it like my mother's belly is a map to a blind person and the doctor is searching. Dr. Sharma moves her stethoscope across silvery striations in my mother's belly for a long time. What is wrong? Why do her fingers keep searching? Is the heartbeat missing?

Oh my god, was my mother right about spirits taking the baby? I back away. I don't want to see my mother's face when Dr. Sharma tells her. I am pressed up to the door, and my heart is racing. I want to throw her clothes at her and say, "Now, Mom. Let's go," so we don't have to hear the words.

Dr. Sharma's bracelets chime. She straightens. "Yes, yes, he is dropping. Do not forget to take the iron. Iron prevents a woman from becoming anemic. Keep your blood strong for this big boy."

This big boy. He's not stillborn?

The relief washes through me as I stand still by the door and my mother pulls down her shirt, fumbles her way into her boots. I have become too close to these people. My heart is racing from worrying about the fingertips traveling up and down the silver rivers. Any day, they will leave! Baby, grandmother, all. And I will be as if I never existed because I've let my existence get wrapped up in theirs.

SECRETS THAT MUST BE TOLD

Back home, my mother is explaining how a girl can get pregnant. She says, "It can happen if moonlight crosses the water."

"Ohhhhhh," Yiey says. Now we understand the power of Bong Proh. The light path of the moon. My grandmother does not find this amusing because she knows more about the Bong guy. Once she said he won't give the baby money, but still my mother needed to leave.

I turn to go. I've done what I said I would do for my mother.

My mother says, "I am still worried for this baby. Don't make the ancestors mad at me. I have such bad karma. I'm so scared for this boy."

"You're scared for this baby because of ancestors?" I say. I hope my voice shows the contempt and anger I want to feel. I hope it hurts her. At the same time I think about the chant Yiey said while she composed the shrine. I asked her to translate. She said, *Whatever I do, to that I will fall heir.* Karma. "The monks chant it," she had said.

"Each one is connected, person to person, ancestor to us," my mother says.

She tries to sit with her belly to one side. "From the time I was small, I've had very bad karma. And then the ghosts came for you.

That's why I'm a bad mother. I bring bad luck for my child. That's why Johnny has to raise you."

I don't understand. I can't grasp what she's saying. I don't want to. I'm done.

"Because of what *you* did?" I am putting on my coat.

She nods.

"And now they want this baby boy. I have very bad karma." That's all she can tell me.

"What'd you do to cause bad karma?" I say. "You don't make any sense."

"She beg her brother," Yiey says, "She beg him all the time. She say, 'My stomach hurt. Please, Rithy.'"

"The boy who got the crickets?" I say.

"I don't know," my mother mumbles.

Yiey says, "Srey Pov, she is three years younger than her brother."

"That is why you have bad karma?" I pull my cap low, bracing to open the door.

She points at the baby inside her. "Him, too. What will protect this baby? There's not only a river but an ocean to take him." She doesn't want to talk anymore. She goes to the kitchen and puts the kettle on.

If I stay I will only start picking for a fight.

I can't bear myself. I hate that I care that the doctor kept listening for the baby's heartbeat. I hate that I care that it might be dead.

My biggest fear: I'll come home one day to this house and they'll all be gone. Not a trace.

So I hate *them*. All over again. Still. But I haven't left yet.

Then my grandmother tells me, "They beat my son for stealing cricket. They put bag on Rithy head and tie him to the mango tree until he stop breathing. They say, no one touch this person. He selfish. All food is for Angkar—government. They tell us, Angkar look after you, brother, sister, mother, father. But we starve."

I stand motionless.

She has terrified me. I have her blood. I have the little boy's blood. *Each one is connected person to person, ancestor to us.*

"I don't want you for ancestors. I don't want that story." I have stopped shouting like them, but I have that story. It flashes bright, like a monk in his saffron-colored robe in New Hampshire snow. The thin legs of the boy. The mango tree that would have no fruit.

"You let them put a bag on his head?" I say to my grandmother. "He was your son."

"Rithy was five years old," my mother says. This is the first time she has said his name. "They said that if anyone touched him, if anyone cried, they would get the bag, too. They kill you if you cry."

I absorb her words. I think of a five-year-old boy, little legs running, very good at hunting crickets. Starving children pouncing on the knot of crickets in his scarf. He fed his little sister, Srey Pov.

If Rithy was five, Srey Pov, little sister, my mother, would have been two years old.

LOST

I'm not late when I arrive at work. This doesn't take the scowl from Vincent's lips.

The day is slightly longer. I carry with me the image of my mother's body warming Pilot in the thawing earth. The story of Rithy curls in my stomach.

Vincent's on special drinks, I'm on the register. He keeps up a banter between orders.

"Got held up in traffic on the 95 bridge. Till five o'clock."

"What happened?"

"I was at Kittery Trading Post . . ."

"Tell me what happened on the bridge?" I touch his sleeve. I think of the helicopters.

"Some kind of accident. I was back a ways."

"Was somebody hurt?"

I hear them, the helicopters plying the river.

People stand in line, and I try to hear them. But I'm on the bridge in my imagination. The river below would be shimmering. I've seen the drop to the river. It is forever, the distance down, what do you think about as you spin? Do you open your arms and fly?

"But then we got going again," Vincent says. "Who knows what happened? Sometimes traffic stops cold, backs up a mile, and you never know why."

I stop listening to Vincent and come back into this space, become aware of customers, with their pained looks. A text comes through. I sneak a glance at my phone. It's Luke, asking when I'll come. I freeze. Shut my eyes. He's waiting for me. Everything's okay.

"Hop to it. I know you can do it." Vincent's on the warpath, marching up and down from the bins to the drive-up. "Don't have my ears on. You gotta yell."

Pilot's in the car. I brought her so I can leave. Right from here. I have everything.

"Hi, what can I get for you?" I do have my earpiece on, and I return to the steady, rushed, insistent voices that come through the ears at the drive-up. "Medium dark roast caramel swirl. Anything else?"

"Hand that latte to the nice lady in the blue shirt," from Vincent. "What can I get for you guys?"

"Gonna need you longer tonight," he says to me while he prepares the next lattes. "We got to mop behind the coolers, and it's not going to happen with this rush till we close."

"Vincent." I shake my head. The line is out the door. A woman keeps repeating her order in my ear. "Sausage and egg no cheese croissant and an iced latte." "I can't!" I say. The woman in my ear says, "Why not?"

Vincent says, "Won't take long."

I'm numb with anger.

On break I go to Pilot in the car, sleeping with my backpack. I have slipped out repeatedly and covered her with two old blankets, but she thinks she's being punished. Pilot cries, she is so happy I came back. I start the engine to get some heat in the truck, and she slides her nose through my bent arm and cries. It's too cold.

I text Luke. *10.*

I look up at the orange donut sign. It seems to radiate.

My eyes fill with fat globs of tears. I smear them away with the blanket. Pilot climbs in my lap. I tell her, "You're a Georgia girl, you shouldn't have to be this cold." We look at the orange light. I ask her, "Who is this Rithy boy? Who is this Srey Pov?" They are telling folk stories. And I don't want to go home.

Maybe it's time for Luke and me. Maybe I need to go.

I call my father's number while I fix my ponytail and my cap. I need to get back.

"Dad," I say.

"Sofie," he says.

"Is this you?" I say.

"All that's left," he says. "Bruiser of a day."

I shut my eyes. I miss him so much. I want to tell him, slowly, *I am going to Luke's tonight, remember Luke who crewed for you*? He is too far away to stop me. I just want to tell him, like I used to tell him everything. So it's not a secret. I want to tell him I know the story I don't want to know.

Instead, I talk about food.

"What do you eat? Do you miss my chowder?"

"You bet. Look, I got to get going. Can I call you in the morning?"

"What did you eat tonight?"

"This woman next door fried us chicken."

From Chincoteague, a man shouts, a dog barks. "Have to go," my father says.

"Dad," I say. "Why do you call me the rabbit in the moon?"

"Something your mother used to say," he says. "Something about Buddha. Maybe good luck. We take every drop of luck we can get."

"I thought you told me that."

"In the morning," he says.

I keep the phone to my ear for a little longer. Just the phone.

The orange light shines down like the moon. And I remember the Cambodian lullaby I made up, "My family rides in the curve of the moon."

I sneak Pilot in the back door of the store and warm her. I give her my boot.

MARCH 1

I wake in Luke's bed. I hear birds as loud as bells. Luke is asleep.

I know this in the dark. I look out the window of the cabin and see an enormous full moon. I rise and feel the chill of the room. It's winter, and I realize there are no birds. The birds are in my mind.

What if we go away from here? From the ocean. Last night's question flickers.

I race to the bathroom and back, out of the cold and into the warmth of the bed.

If he would hold me, the fear I have this morning will pass. I bury myself inside the covers. Luke and I are identical crystals in a frozen pane of glass. Then, I do something I shouldn't. But anyone might. I don't wake him before I do this. I don't warn him. I tuck myself around the curve of his back.

In that instant time stops.

I know this was not supposed to happen, but I also know it could not have been prevented. I know it's no one's fault.

Luke flips and lunges at me. In that instant I hear a roar like I've never heard. He grabs me around the chest. Suddenly I'm on my back, locked under his knee. It happens too fast for me to call out. I can't breathe. I pound him. I think I pound the bones of his back. And then I scream out when an opening comes in my throat. I push with all my strength on his shoulders. "Luke!"

In a flash he's in this place, in the cabin. He knows everything. His hands drop like I'm an ember, I'm orange fire.

I suck air back into my lungs. I'm crouched on the floor with nothing on. He's beside me. He covers me in the blanket. I feel his arms try to hold me and lift me. My body pulls away from him. "I am so cold," I say.

I stand, still breathing deliberately. He reaches for me. I hear an awful sound. It makes me turn to him. He is crying. I don't know what to do, so I put on my clothes. Soon I'll have to do something, but I focus on the work of my hands. On buttons, on the laces of my boots.

Luke turns away. I watch him pull on his shirt, then his sweater. It's still dark.

"Let's get out of here," he says.

A phrase Luke had spoken somehow comes through my mind. Golden hour. I think of the golden hour. That hour after a trauma. You have one hour when you can alter events. One hour when things can change. Start a heart that's stopped beating. Staunch a hemorrhage.

I let out a long cry, "Oh, Luke." And when I see his shoulders, how his arms simply hang, I know that he knows it too.

But what do we do? I remember the gun and vaguely think I need to get rid of it. Why didn't I get rid of it when I first knew where it was?

I go and press his shoulder. He needs to turn around.

I am in my jeans, my combat boots. The baseball cap my father gave me. We walk from the cabin and down the dirt road. It's natural to walk toward the small house in the curve of the road by the breakwater, where we've walked before. The cold air fills my chest and burns. We are ordinary people walking. Aren't we?

It's high water. It beats against the breakwater where we stop.

I lift the gun I brought with us.

He stops. He didn't see me grab it as he dressed.

I had imagined I'd show it to him, since we can't talk about it. At least I'd get it in the open. But I want to know how it feels if I hold it with both of my hands.

"I found where you hid it. One day I was reading your book."

Luke doesn't reach for it. Past the gun, I see his chest lift and fall. He's a soldier. He knows a million tricks to take this gun I barely hold upright. But he doesn't.

"Sofie," he says.

The gun is cold against my bare skin.

"What are you doing?" he says.

"I don't know," I say, "I was always scared you'd hurt yourself. I hate this gun."

I'm aware of the moon. It fills the sky behind me. I turn to the side so I can keep it in my sight. From the ocean comes the unrelenting rhythm of a foghorn. I hold the gun with both hands, but the moon distracts me. I think I see the shape of a rabbit with his legs outstretched.

What an amazing sight, to see a rabbit run across the moon. Luke must see it, too, because he begins to talk to me in the voice I know as his. He doesn't just disappear like he did from his family. He is here.

"No surprises. Warn me, Sofie." His steadiness returns. We know what we're doing. "I told you." Again, "No surprises. Do you think I'll hurt you?" he says.

I shake my head. "I know," I say. I still hold the gun.

"Come back to the cottage."

"I know," I say again.

"It will never happen again," he says. We both are certain this is true.

"I want to fire it," I say.

He studies the shoreline, the harbor.

“Not here,” he says.

We are so reasonable.

We get in the car. He drives us south to a desolate stretch of dunes that is now ridges of sand and snow. “You want to fire, fire here.”

We walk to the end of a point of land. Ahead is only wind and crashing waves. Luke is beside me. He pulls the slide back on the gun so it’s cocked. Places it in my hands. I hold the gun the way I held my father’s gun. My left hand wraps around my firing hand, my thumbs crossing. I aim for the waves. My finger wraps around the trigger. Hold my breath. I pull. I’m aware of the blast the gun makes. I anticipated the blast. But I had held the gun so tightly that I feel my hands pop up in the air.

I step back and steady myself. I disengage the magazine.

Then I throw the gun with all my weight through the wind, and it’s lost in the sea.

SURVIVORS

He drives. I slide down in the passenger seat, watching the sun's light beginning to disrupt the dark from under the bill of my Mason Oil cap. The gun blast still feels terribly good. I can't explain. He reaches across and takes my hand. I take his. We drive back to the cottage. Pilot is at the door, waiting, but it's too early, and she settles back down by the stove. I put on my dog tags, my hip-long sweater; I brush my hair at a tiny mirror over the sink.

I still have streaks of Spanish green around my eyes. Luke stands with his back to me, facing the ocean. He turns. He's wearing a Greetings from Hampton Beach T-shirt, the shirt he sleeps in sometimes.

I focus on the shirt, but he is saying something. I don't want to listen. I know where we're going. He says, "You and I are always going to have a gun."

I stand like I did the first time I stayed, my palms against the wood of the door behind me.

I look into his tortured eyes. I know what he means. It's in our history and will always be part of our story.

"You're gonna break my heart if I ask you to stay," he says, "if we stay together. We need to take care of ourselves. First."

The *first* saves me.

He comes to me and places his hand on my back. I feel his fingers and hand press up my spine, like zipping a tight, tight dress.

I say, "Where will you go?"

He shrugs. "The place my family talks about."

"The place out west with river rapids."

"Yes."

"Maybe you could sleep," I say, about out west.

He shoves his hair off his forehead. "Could stop by home."

I wrap my arm around his ribs.

He wraps his arm around mine.

I also see Yiey's face as she looks at us. It is tender.

The foghorn sounds. And again. And again. He straightens. The smell of the incense in my little shrine, although it's not lit, is sharp and sweet.

I want to make plans with him. Call me. In one week. In six months. In seven years like you said. I say, "You'll see your little sister. Mandy." Maybe we both have a flash of her smile. I wipe tears off my face with both of my hands. He turns away.

I'm trying to leave him, but I have to tell him . . . I start to laugh and bend down and feel my hair fall down over me.

"You're laughing."

"I know you need to go. I know I need to leave you. But my crazy grandmother's here."

"She's always here," he says.

"Just let me say this. Something about being with you," I say slowly, "helps me—makes me—look at my family. The crazy ones."

"They're not crazy," he says.

Like us? I wonder.

He's trying to help me go. He lifts my head. "We're like this, your grandmother and me," he says, holding up two fingers, tight, and I smile at him. "We tell stories like a couple lifers. I'm working on getting her into the bar at the VFW." For a second I imagine my grandmother in her T-shirt and sarong wrapped around her hips on a bar stool with Vietnam vets and guys back from Iraq and Afghanistan.

"Sophea," he says. "Strong girl."

We look at each other.

This is the golden hour.

Tears are streaming down my cheeks. Pilot is curled in a ball by the stove. I put on my plaid jacket and cap. He watches.

"Pilot," I whisper. She's on her feet and to the door. Luke doesn't stop me, but he doesn't let me. He holds me with his eyes until I have my dog.

Pilot and I step into the snow.

Outside I bend over in grief. What have I done?

I look up at the moon. I force myself to follow it along the ocean.

COD

My truck crunches on iced-over snow, traveling onto Ocean Boulevard under the early morning sky. I am almost unable to see the road through my tears. I haven't seen a car yet. No one expects me, except Mr. Murray. Vincent doesn't expect me. My father doesn't expect me. Not my mother. If she remembers, she thinks I'm heading to school with Rosa, who will know where I was. Not Luke. It's just me and my dog.

I ride along the ocean past Rye Harbor, where my mother met my father, Wallis Sands, Wentworth by the Sea where Mr. Murray had his honeymoon, New Castle Common, the bridges from New Castle to Portsmouth. I find myself pulling in at the co-op, an old habit.

I step down from the truck, red eyed, blowing my nose. Pete's here, at his boat. "What's going on, kid? What's wrong? No school?"

"Hey, Pete. Oh, hay fever, something."

He says, "Hay fever. Yeah? It's early March. Come on, kid."

I go and sit on his dock by his boat, *Cat o' Nine Tails.* He's got a thermos of bitter brew coffee, and he pours me a small plastic lid full. He sits in the cabin among old bags of chips, stacks of bad movies, Kilim cups enough to wade through. I am happy to see him. I start to bawl.

"That hay fever," he says.

"I miss my father," I say. I am still wearing the baseball cap.

"Yeah," he says again. "What kind of work is this, takes your father away?"

I shake my head, sobbing, but trying to drink this wicked bad coffee. "Do you have any milk?" I manage to say.

"Try these Mallomars," he says and digs up a really old box of the chocolate-covered marshmallow cookies I haven't had since I was six. I take one, dip it in the coffee, keep crying. Pete doesn't know what to say, so he starts talking cod.

"You know, it's cod I worry about," Pete says. "No cod. Used to rain cod. I dream them. All I ever wanted to do was fish. It's a game of chance. Like the arcade games up to the beach. All I ever wanted. I'll go out for monkfish if I can find them. I'll go out till I die. Going to be about four boats left fishing out of New Hampshire."

I take short, gaspy breaths. I begin to drink the coffee with melted marshmallow and listen to the old story I know.

"You buy shares of a fish for a buck fifty a pound. Got to pay the fuel, pay the boat, pay the crew. So if on the day I land the fish, they're bringing ninety-nine cents a pound, I'm in debt before I begin. That's the game. Every card's a wild card."

"Pete, when you go, could I crew?"

"Well, sure," he says. "But girl, you'd have to get on the boat. Are you changing your ways?"

"Don't know, Pete. I don't know anything. I just didn't want you to go out alone."

"Hard with a girl. You got to have a bucket." Pete's an old-timer.

"If I get on a boat, I'll figure that part out," I say. "You still dream cod?"

"Every night," he says.

"Please don't stop talking, Pete."

"You got it bad," he says.

I lay my head on the dock by his feet.

RIVER

"Sophea?"

"Yes!" I say, startled. I know the voice instantly. The one who has always called me Sophea.

Pilot and I had wrapped up in all the extra blankets when Pete left for breakfast and said I could stay right there if I wanted. I hear Luke say, *You can't hesitate. You have to be ready every second. You have to act or you're gonna lose a soldier. He's gonna bleed out or his heart's gonna stop if you're not on it.* Am I ever going to not remember all the things he told me?

"Sophea," again, commanding.

I make myself open my eyes and face the new light. My grandmother is leaning down in the silver morning. I see the cloth of her skirt beneath her heavy snow coat. And I see the distinct bones of her face and wide lips and sharp eyes. I am not afraid.

Around us the water is black.

She says, "Now we go fishing."

"Fishing?" I say. She wants to board Pete's boat.

"Help me get in," she says.

"We're not going fishing."

The tide holds the boat a few feet beneath the level of the pier. She is shaky on one foot, the other trying to step down. She is determined to board, and instinctively I steady her body as she boards the *Cat o' Nine Tails.*

"Yiey, how did you get here? I'll take you back."

"We go on river. When I was a girl, before the Pol Pot time, I fish on the river. Tonle Sap."

"This river is not still. This river can kill you, its current."

"Many thing can kill you. Now we fish."

I hear heels on the pier. Light and musical. Not the *clomp clomp* of fishermen's boots. "Rosa bring me," Yiey says, and suddenly here is Rosa on the pier. Rosa's face is like a sunbeam. I reach up to hug her. I smell her Nirvana cologne from Prelude. Even in the foggy dawn Rosa smells like Nirvana.

"Rosa! She wants to go fishing. Tell her I never go on the river."

"Well," Rosa says, "you can't take *this* boat. You don't have a license, and your father would have to pay another fine."

But Yiey points to the tiny rowboat Pete uses to row to the fishing boat if he has to tie up off the pier.

"I never go on the river," I say again. My heart is pounding. We are in slack water. But I know the water can overcome and can wash a body out to sea. "Why?" I say.

"To catch magic fish for Srey Pov."

I look out on the black river. I believe the river holds magic, too. "Rosa, can Pilot stay with you?" I look at her and see she's carrying Yiey's fishing pole. "Why should I trust you?" I say to Yiey. "You don't know this river."

She says, "You know this river. Like Rithy know that field."

I think of Rithy hunting crickets. I touch the dog tags pressed against my chest. I have an opening—it's a secret opening—I have some opening in me for Rithy, who must not have slept, either, waiting for the soldier's footsteps. If Rithy comes through that opening to me, well, who's that baby sister he comes bringing by the hand?

I stand by Rosa on the pier. It's Rosa and me and the fishing pole. Yiey is checking out Pete's boat. "Why'd you bring her?" I whisper. "Did they know I didn't stay with you?"

"What do you think?" And we look at Yiey in the boat and we know there was no choice if Yiey called. Yiey is a force of nature. And the river has magic. And I am shaking with fear.

"You broke it off," Rosa says. "You look different."

I shake my head at her. A shake that says, simply, yes.

"We knew you came here," she says. "Everybody knows Johnny's truck."

I step from the dock, down the ladder, into the small boat that rests in slack water. The boat heels with my imbalanced step. Then Yiey steps down. We sit hard on the strips of wood that serve as seats. Rosa hands Yiey her pole.

Yiey and I are knees to knees.

My father goes out at slack water, when there is little stress between the ebb current and the flood current. Maybe I can do this, take Yiey for magic fish.

I know how to row. Hadn't I seen it done a million times? I row the little boat slowly from between the berthed fishing boats and onto the river. I see the flash of Rosa's yellow light from the pier.

The tide lifts us. I feel like I'm rowing into another world, but I hold on with my mind to Rosa's light as long as I can. I know the river. I know its curves. I know the rock where seals haul out to bask in sunlight, the rock that Pete ground into and ripped off the hull. I know the river's snake that slashes down the center.

My arms pull strong. At first we glide. The river doesn't resist the work of my oars.

I know we must go to the deepest water where schools of fish feed, away from the shore. I can feel my heart pound as we come full into the river.

Then we get sucked into what feels like a funnel and it spins us around and I believe Yiey and I have given ourselves to the whims of the current. I don't lose my grip on the oars, but I hold on to Yiey with my eyes. Her eyes are vigilant but not afraid. When the spin slows, I pull the oars through the water. I feel the surge as I pull.

The current spits us into an eddy. A sweet eddy. Far away are the rocky banks of Peirce Island. We have crossed the center. Above, the looming walls of the old navy prison shimmer, and it turns into a castle in the morning light.

Yiey drops her line in the river that leads to the sea. I think of my father's stop, the one he always told Rosa and me about. There's a stop in the sea where you can pick up anything you need.

I am on the water and I can still breathe. The blackness surrounds us. I have the oars in my hands. I finesse the power of the current, hanging our small boat in the eddy.

Yiey methodically reels in her line. At first she is gray in the dim light. Then she is in color. I see the yellow and green of her skirt. Her black hair knotted at the back of her neck. The gulls are quiet, and then they lift and swoop their wings wide, little groans in their throats as they touch down to the water.

Yiey reels in a blue-black sea bass. She holds on to the pole with strong hands, not at all concerned with the heft of him. We see his pale belly as she reels him in. He is large enough, she says. One is magic enough. She drops him in her bucket.

"Okay," she says. "Okay."

We turn. I row and feel the power of my arms as I pull. A small smile is on Yiey's lips. When I find Rosa's light, I follow it across the spine of the river and bring our small boat back to shore.

Pilot yelps with joy and hunger—it's way past breakfast—to see us come back. On the dock, my body still rocks with the sea, but I look out to where I rowed. "We came back," I say to Yiey. She is matter-of-fact, busy with her fishing pole, securing the fish. "Now we cook," she says.

I look out. All that space out there. Maybe that is mine. Maybe Luke will explore, too, and what holds him will lose some of its power.

THE SOLDIER NOT HERE

Yiey has filleted the fish and fries it in a skillet. She says that if you dream a baby, it means a baby will come live with you.

"The soldier not here," she says.

I think of both the little Pol Pot boy with the ax and Luke Sanna at Rye Harbor. I shake my head. "He is not here." I step away. They are both not here. I close my eyes. I stretch my body across Luke's in my mind.

Yiey brings a piece of the fish to my mother, who has dark half circles under her eyes. She's not sleeping. My mother breaks it into bites and slowly brings each bite to her mouth. My grandmother and I watch the movement of her hand and her mouth.

My grandmother pulls the red kitchen chair in front of us, sits with one hand on each of our thighs. Strong hand, patting.

"She is good karma, this one," my grandmother says.

I feel the weight of her body press against my knee. "Me?" I say, surprised. "I have good karma?"

She cocks her head with her lips pressed slightly together.

"Maybe," she says. "You help me remember when I was a girl and we catch magic fish."

Because of Luke, I think, I could go on the water and bring back a fish.

I feel the ache of my arms from pulling against the water.

My mother eats her fill of the fish, and I think of the doctor calling the baby "big boy." He'll probably grow up with a craving for sea bass caught in March from the middle of the river. Where is Luke? What do I do with the stories I told only him?

YOU SING

"You need fresh air," I tell my mother. "You need rosiness in your cheeks." She is large and glum and exhausted looking and sallow, as well. "Maybe it's good looking for berries in the woods." She achieves a half smile.

Then I tell her, "I missed you all the time. I had this song I sang to you." I say this without emotion to my mother.

We are silent. Our hands are busy folding warm clothes from the dryer.

"You sing," Yiey says.

I shrug, sing a few lines.

Ma sings to me, her long hair flowing.

I love her more than the dark loves dawn.

I don't go on. This is as close as we will come to expressing affection. It would also be true to shout, I've *always* always hated you.

"Your mother come here to stay because I say. She want to, but she scare. It is bad karma to not take care your kid. No matter how hard your life, you have to take care your kid."

Yiey likes the house very hot. I am wearing only a T-shirt and leggings. With my father, we kept the heat so low, we bundled in sweaters, sometimes snow pants. But Yiey said, too cold.

My grandmother rubs my back. Her fingers are strong.

"I remember the rabbit," I say. "From my childhood. I thought my father told the rabbit story, but he said it was you. About looking for the rabbit in the moon. I was happy when I looked for it."

My mother shakes her head. "A children's story. When you were little, I told you, look up there at the moon. See the rabbit? I would roll a ball of sticky rice and pop it in your mouth. You would stare and stare, and chew the rice and look for the rabbit."

"It made me happy," I say again.

"It a Buddha story," Yiey says. "One time the Buddha is a rabbit. The rabbit have no food to give the god, so he throw himself on the fire. He give himself. The god thought, this rabbit is loyal. He make the fire grow cold and the rabbit not die, and the god paint his picture on the moon. And now the rabbit on the moon and he is stirring pot, a potion that he drink and he live forever. That a true story."

"You mean immortality?" I say.

"Yeah," my grandmother says. "The rabbit on the moon is about ancestor and how the Buddha honor them. He make them live forever."

I think of Rithy. Now I hold him, too, like my mother and grandmother. I have his story.

My family rides in the curve of the moon.

Luke would like this story. Maybe the ghosts would be more content and settle into their old bones and Luke would sleep.

"Mom, I'm hungry," I say. Relieved to not talk anymore, she waddles to the kitchen. She begins rice in the cooker. Soon the house smells like basmati rice. While it cooks, she brings my grandmother and me bowls of hot tom yum soup with tamarind broth. I sit cross-legged on the couch and slurp it down. Then my mother brings steaming rice with red chilies and spring rolls we dip in green mango sauce; she pours from a pot of jasmine tea. We're not done.

She brings us a platter of bananas fried golden in batter.

We sit back, all of us with our hands on our bellies.

It feels like the first whole meal I've eaten with my mother since I was five. My belly is full.

"If you see the rabbit in the moon you are blessed," my mother says. She believes this bodes well for the new one.

But no sooner have we eaten than her contractions start. "Maybe they won't do the C-section if he wants to come now," my mother says through grimaces. Yiey puts on her coat over her sarong, and we pack up to go. Then we ride three abreast in the truck to go to the hospital. The moon comes with us, too.

I imagine many things in the moon. A bump for a pot, a crack for an ear. The rabbit stirring the potion of immortality.

LUCKY BOY

I am holding Heng, "lucky boy." My father drives back to New Hampshire, both he and his deckhand, who wants to see his kid. My father comes to help us. He lectures my mother, his first wife, like she's my older sister. "Don't go back to that guy. He's poison for you." He tells her there's an apartment in Newmarket a buddy of Pete's is trying to rent. He tells her. She nods, like a teenager, looking at help wanteds on my computer.

My father takes over the couch by the woodstove. His boat's in Virginia, but he stays a while and fishes a few days here with Pete.

Heng and I are surrounded by every plastic infant product sold in America. All the Cambodians in New England have come to see Heng, bringing a plastic bathtub, car seat, baby rocker, baby crawler, high chair, hammer toy, a mobile of tiny giraffes that plays him songs in the crib.

Heng is too tiny to believe. He does one thing very well. Eat. He loves to eat. Pilot stares in amazement and abject envy. Pilot has to wait for sunrise and sunset to eat. This creature, so little a fisherman would have to toss him back for another season's growing if he were a fish, eats around the clock.

My grandmother is soaking spring roll wrappers.

I put the baby, who finally fell asleep, in one of his plastic bassinettes. I have printed out various forms for my business plan project at school. Now I'm filling out federal permit forms, state forms, all the forms for a CSF.

My father shakes his head at the forms.

"By the books," I tell him. "By every book the government wrote."

"If you got the heart for it," he says.

My mother signs the forms. I ask her because she is over twenty-one. She does this solemnly.

"We got dogged," my father says to my mother, Rosa, and me one day when he comes home from fishing. We are working on forms at the kitchen table. "Net full of them." He means dogfish.

He and Pete truck what monkfish they caught down to Gloucester. I know he gutted the monkfish on board. They are the ugliest fish in the world, but the reason he guts them isn't because no one should have to see how ugly they are. The ugly head and dagger teeth are half the body, but he guts them because the meat is in the tail so the tail is all they bring in.

Rosa says she and her mom will kitchen test some good dogfish recipes and we could make dogfish a delicacy if we open a CSF in the summer. Sweet New Hampshire dogfish. She's also imagining small concerts we could do beside our CSF. A girl band would build extreme excitement, she says, and draw people to our market.

Now Rosa's in. We don't know what to call our CSF, so we ask my grandmother, "What should the name be?"

She does not wonder. She says, "Magic Fish."

"We'll call it Magic Fish CSF, Portsmouth."

"*Do you like fish?*" Rosa says, trying out a marketing plan. "*Buy it Fresh from the Boat. Support Seacoast Fishermen. Today's recipe: Sweet Dogfish Marsala.*

"We'll get a map of the Gulf of Maine to show where Johnny

goes, and we'll also have never-ending recipes for cooking the tail of a monkfish. *Tastes like lobster!*"

My father watches Heng in my mother's arms. My father is thin as a tree and bronzed. That's what Chincoteague did to him. Heng is jowly. He wears incredibly tiny Mickey Mouse sneakers from Auntie Rosa. I lean over to the baby and wipe his fat lips that pooch out sideways while he sleeps.

He wakes, and my father holds him for a while, but when Heng's lips start to crinkle and before he can let out a cry, my father hands the baby to my mother. Pilot stands by whoever holds him, and when he sleeps, Pilot lies beneath his baby crib, her head on her paw, waiting.

LOVE SONG

I stand alone by the window in Mr. Murray's room and watch the tug that has been guiding that same tanker up the river all semester.

At seven thirty Mr. Murray walks in. He wears a white scarf around his neck, the same white as his beard, which I think he has trimmed. He looks at me and nods his head, like he assumed, of course, Sofie Grear could be here.

"I just want to know," I say. "Have you read *Maggie Cassidy*?"

"Beautiful story," he says, taking off his scarf. "A love song to Lowell. A love song to Jack Kerouac's people. Have you read it?"

"My friend Luke and I read it. And we read it to each other, different scenes."

I don't say how sometimes we read it stretched across his bed, and sometimes we put it down to kiss.

"Thank you, Mr. Murray."

"Any time, Ms. Grear."

I go to my locker.

Good. That felt good. Just to touch Luke in that tiny way feels *so* good.

PEIRCE ISLAND

Pilot and I drive to the spit of land where she loves to race the birds, out beyond the Fisherman's Co-op. She races. I walk the length of the small island and stand at a semicircle of rocks overlooking the dogleg of the river. A breeze lifts from the river. Looking west, I see the Memorial Bridge, the Sarah Long Bridge, and in the distance my bridge, the arch rising over I-95.

Across the river, cranes at the Navy Yard lift at an angle to the sky. If I stayed till sunset I'd hear the bugle call. Not Taps. But in my mind I can hear Luke whistling it for my grandmother, and I can imagine the notes coming across the river from the shipyard sound system. The memory of the sound fills me, and I see Luke at the window, whistling the notes to the words I always add.

> Day is done,
> Gone the sun,
> From the hills, from the lakes, from the skies.
> All is well,
> Safely rest,
> God is nigh.

The notes press on my heart.

"He will chase the ghost," Yiey had said. "He help Srey Pov.

He need time to take care himself."

I look out over the rocks. Sometimes I see seals even in winter. They could be rocks until I see their eyes staring back. Souls of the drowned. Luke had hope in the seals and their mysteries, imagining how a living creature can transform and endure.

I call Pilot. She is busy, her licorice tail pointing, her right paw lifted, as she finds me a bird. I call again. She releases. We race with the wind round the curve of the land.

Rosa catches up with us, and we walk in the pebbles down on the beach before I go in to work. It's mid March, and already the air's different. It doesn't cut into my skin.

"I missed your opening at the Press Room," I say.

"I was breathtaking," Rosa says. "I'm officially a country western star. I wore boots with five-inch heels."

Rosa has small Mickey Mouses painted on her fingernails over coral-pink polish. Her hair is down today and curled around her face.

"I did come to your birthday," she says.

"Thank you," I say.

"How is seventeen?"

I will remember seventeen as the year that I found it easy to slide into *Maggie Cassidy* and grasp a gun in my hand. And fire it into the Atlantic Ocean. And I loved a soldier.

"Seventeen," I say. "I was a Spanish dancer."

STICKY RICE

It's another work day. Soon I'll I step into Dunkin' Donuts, *Keeps You Running.*

Vincent will say, "Good of you."

The orders will start coming through my earpiece. Vincent's tattooed fingers will dance on the register.

From the couch I see the mailman come up the walk. He's got a package way too big to put in the slot. At the door he hands it to me—an oversized mailer, bumpy and as long as Yiey's bass.

It's addressed to me.

I look at it a long time, still standing at the door. The baby is asleep. My mother is wearing a blue sarong and is preparing sticky rice. She has put the steam pot on to boil. When it boils, I know she'll drain the sticky rice in the bamboo steam basket, then rest the basket over the boiling water in the pot.

I put on my plaid jacket over my sweatshirt, the one that I always wear now with my Mason Oil cap. Luke would tease me and say I look like I work in a gas station.

I take the envelope outside. The small skiff is on its side by the chimney. I right it so its flat bottom is in the snow, which is down to only a foot or so. I step inside the skiff and sit. Lift the hood of the sweatshirt over my cap. I turn the package all around. It has no return address.

I peel the tape and rip the perforated seal. What's inside is wrapped in a layer of heavy brown paper. And under that, a layer of sheer paper, like tracing paper. When I get to the sheer paper, my hands start to shake. I can see.

I let the brown paper fall, then lift the picture, painted on cardboard, from its thin sleeve.

Luke has sent his painting of the medic with his fingers on the pulse of the child. There's the jagged splotches of polish on the child's nails. He has added something. I still can't see their faces, only the downward turn of the medic's head, the black and white American flag. But now, in the little girl's fist is a lollipop, pale cream with swirls of pink and turquoise, a little bit chewed on already. She's holding it firmly, upright.

He said, *We never know what happens, we move on.* But with the swirling lollipop he added, the story seems to shift. Maybe the child has a chance for healing. Maybe now the picture has hope.

My mother is still cooking. She is barefoot. I see her small steps as she moves from the stove to the sink. It's a tiny kitchen, and she moves back and forth. It becomes like a dance, step toe, step back, step toe, pause, or lift on her toes as she needs to reach something.

I unlace my boots and take off my socks and step onto the kitchen linoleum beside her.

She puts her finger to her lips. I nod.

She shakes the rice to loosen it in the bamboo basket. I take the basket and flip the rice to steam on the other side. Yiey taught me. She slices a mango, which she'll serve on the sweet rice. We open the lids of the individual serving baskets. Six baskets in a row on the counter. I imagine how Luke would paint them, the baskets in the morning light, the bright orange of the mango.

As we work, my bare feet move across the floor like my mother's.